**"BUT WHAT ABOUT THE CONTRACT?
ARE YOU READY TO SIGN?"**

"Not on your life, boss lady," he said with a bold grin as he moved toward the door. "We've just begun to negotiate. You've made your offer, but I have a few ideas of my own about the terms."

"Want to tell me what they are?" she asked, following him to the door.

"No way," he said softly. "We wouldn't want the game to end this easily, would we?"

Before Kelly realized what he intended, he leaned down and kissed her gently. But what began so innocently swiftly became charged with a degree of electricity that brought Kelly swaying toward Grant. She might have fallen had he not caught her in his strong arms and crushed her against his chest, a soft moan escaping him as his lips possessed hers with undeniable hunger and desire.

A CANDLELIGHT ECSTASY ROMANCE ®

162 VIDEO VIXEN, *Elaine Raco Chase*
163 BRIAN'S CAPTIVE, *Alexis Hill Jordan*
164 ILLUSIVE LOVER, *Jo Calloway*
165 A PASSIONATE VENTURE, *Julia Howard*
166 NO PROMISE GIVEN, *Donna Kimel Vitek*
167 BENEATH THE WILLOW TREE, *Emma Bennett*
168 CHAMPAGNE FLIGHT, *Prudence Martin*
169 INTERLUDE OF LOVE, *Beverly Sommers*
170 PROMISES IN THE NIGHT, *Jackie Black*
171 HOLD LOVE TIGHTLY, *Megan Lane*
172 ENDURING LOVE, *Tate McKenna*
173 RESTLESS WIND, *Margaret Dobson*
174 TEMPESTUOUS CHALLENGE, *Eleanor Woods*
175 TENDER TORMENT, *Harper McBride*
176 PASSIONATE DECEIVER, *Barbara Andrews*
177 QUIET WALKS THE TIGER, *Heather Graham*
178 A SUMMER'S EMBRACE, *Cathie Linz*
179 DESERT SPLENDOR, *Samantha Hughes*
180 LOST WITHOUT LOVE, *Elizabeth Raffel*
181 A TEMPTING STRANGER, *Lori Copeland*
182 DELICATE BALANCE, *Emily Elliott*
183 A NIGHT TO REMEMBER, *Shirley Hart*
184 DARK SURRENDER, *Diana Blayne*
185 TURN BACK THE DAWN, *Nell Kincaid*
186 GEMSTONE, *Bonnie Drake*
187 A TIME TO LOVE, *Jackie Black*
188 WINDSONG, *Jo Calloway*
189 LOVE'S MADNESS, *Sheila Paulos*
190 DESTINY'S TOUCH, *Dorothy Ann Bernard*
191 NO OTHER LOVE, *Alyssa Morgan*
192 THE DEDICATED MAN, *Lass Small*
193 MEMORY AND DESIRE, *Eileen Bryan*
194 A LASTING IMAGE, *Julia Howard*
195 RELUCTANT MERGER, *Alexis Hill Jordan*
196 GUARDIAN ANGEL, *Linda Randall Wisdom*
197 DESIGN FOR DESIRE, *Anna Hudson*
198 DOUBLE PLAY, *Natalie Stone*
199 SENSUOUS PERSUASION, *Eleanor Woods*
200 MIDNIGHT MEMORIES, *Emily Elliott*
201 DARING PROPOSAL, *Tate McKenna*

DESIRABLE COMPROMISE

Suzanne Sherrill

A CANDLELIGHT ECSTASY ROMANCE ®

Published by
Dell Publishing Co., Inc.
1 Dag Hammarskjold Plaza
New York, New York 10017

ISBN: 0-440-11903-0

Printed in the United States of America
First printing—January 1984

To Our Readers:

We have been delighted with your enthusiastic response to Candlelight Ecstasy Romances®, and we thank you for the interest you have shown in this exciting series.

In the upcoming months we will continue to present the distinctive sensuous love stories you have come to expect only from Ecstasy. We look forward to bringing you many more books from your favorite authors and also the very finest work from new authors of contemporary romantic fiction.

As always, we are striving to present the unique, absorbing love stories that you enjoy most—books that are more than ordinary romance.

Your suggestions and comments are always welcome. Please write to us at the address below.

Sincerely,

The Editors
Candlelight Romances
1 Dag Hammarskjold Plaza
New York, New York 10017

CHAPTER ONE

Kelly shivered in the cool breeze as she stood on the penthouse veranda staring out at the spectacular scene before her. The lights of Chicago were just beginning to sparkle in the twilight sky like the night's first stars. It was a sight that should have thrilled her. Instead, it only served to remind her of the dramatic changes that had taken place in her life in the last few weeks.

Inside the apartment more than one hundred people had gathered to drink the very best Scotch and champagne, to dine on caviar and lobster, all in her honor. Although the evening had been going smoothly enough so far, the tension in that room had been evident and, what's more, Kelly knew the worst was yet to come. She had to work with these people, and while they were being polite enough tonight, she could sense their resentment.

She had begged Lyndon Phillips to allow her to slip quietly into her new position as general manager of his Chicago television station, but he had ignored her plea. This lavish affair had been thrown together with the typically excessive style she had come to expect of the aging Texas millionaire who was her boss. If he had his way, there would probably be a fireworks display with her name emblazoned over the city before the night was over. Lyndon Phillips liked to make an impression, and he'd already demonstrated, merely by hiring her, that surprise was one of his favorite business weapons.

Kelly, at twenty-nine, had been program director of his Dallas station when he'd called her into his office less than two months earlier and announced he had plans for her.

"Kelly, my girl," he'd said with a slow, deliberate drawl, poking his big cigar in the air to emphasize his point, "I like your style. You've got spunk. Just the sort of spunk it'll take to get them bigshots in Chicago off their complacent duffs."

"What are you saying?" she'd asked carefully.

"Young lady, I'm tellin' you I want you to go up there and show them sons a . . . uh, excuse me, them fellows a thing or two about running a television station."

Kelly had been astounded. She had known the job was open. There had been speculation in the trade papers for weeks about who would take over when Ted Randall retired, but she'd had no idea her name was even being considered. Some of the top people in television were after that job and, besides, Lyndon Phillips was considered something of a male chauvinist. The last thing anyone expected was that his choice would be a woman.

The news had taken the industry by storm. It had ruffled a lot of feathers within the Phillips chain, most of them on the predominantly male Chicago staff. The idea of smoothing them had been daunting enough back in Texas, but now, faced with the reality of it in the form of greetings that ranged from distantly polite to blatantly hostile, she could see exactly what she was up against. She shivered again at the thought.

"Cold?" a resonant voice asked, breaking into her reverie.

Kelly looked up into a face that seemed as familiar to her as her own brother's. She had been studying photographs of that face for the last six weeks, trying to attach the string of impressive journalistic credentials and sketchy personal background she'd found in the accompanying résumé to the curiously impersonal expression that had stared back at her. But the glossy black and white publicity photos had not prepared her for the impact of Grant Andrews in person.

What struck Kelly first about the anchorman were his eyes. In the photographs they had seemed light, perhaps blue or possibly gray. Instead, they were an unusual shade of pale green, like a piece of glass washed repeatedly by the sea. Flecked with bits of gold, they reminded her of a cat or, considering the careful examination to which they were subjecting her at the moment, of a panther studying its prey before pouncing. She shivered again.

"You are cold," he said, answering the question she had ignored.

With nonchalant ease he removed his slightly rumpled, lightweight summer sports jacket, which on anyone other than him would have seemed oddly out of place among the dark suits and dinner jackets on this formal occasion. Kelly accepted the jacket gratefully, draping it around her bare shoulders. The tangy scent of his aftershave lingered in the fabric, stirring her senses into a sharp awareness of the man before her.

"It is cooler out here than I'd expected," she admitted.

"No one from Texas ever believes it's possible to have a cool night in the middle of summer," he agreed. "You are the new boss from Dallas, aren't you?"

"Yes. I'm Kelly Patrick," she confirmed, extending her hand. "And you're Grant Andrews."

"Ah, the lady's done her homework," he said approvingly.

"That's how the lady got her job," she countered. "I couldn't be a Boy Scout, but I learned the motto: Be prepared."

"Apparently some of the men who wanted the job missed too many of their scout meetings," he observed wryly. "They were too busy learning to mix a good dry martini."

Falling under the spell of Grant's casual banter, which was a refreshing change from the earlier stilted exchanges with others on the staff, Kelly grinned and retorted, "Even that was wasted, since Lyndon Phillips would never touch a martini." Imitating the Texan's deep drawl, she said, "A man takes his whiskey strong and neat. That other stuff's for women and sissies."

"I see you've made a careful study of Lyndon too," Grant said, laughing with her.

"He was at the top of my list," she said, using the silence that followed to assess the man who was now staring out at the Chicago skyline. She had a feeling he would be far more difficult to comprehend than Lyndon Phillips had been. The Texan, who'd started out poor in a state filled with nouveau riche oilmen, was driven by greed and a desire for power. Nothing in Grant Andrews's file had given Kelly a clue about what drove him. Yet something surely did.

He had started as a street reporter, known for his aggressive tactics and an ability to dig out stories no one else could get. In a matter of months he'd become recognized as the city's most industrious investigative reporter. Five years ago, banking on his growing popularity, the station had moved him into the anchorman's slot. As a concession to getting him to accept the position, he had been allowed to continue to do selected reporting assignments. The station's ratings had climbed steadily from a distant fourth place to number one. No one doubted that Grant Andrews was the reason for the improvement.

Women seemed to find him irresistible, intrigued by his rugged good looks, his cool, impenetrable on-air style, and, no doubt, by his bachelor status. Every poll listed him as one of the city's most eligible and sought-after men. Despite this, men did not seem threatened by him. They approved of his forthright reporting and no-nonsense delivery. They admired his refusal to go along with the happy-talk demeanor that had been in vogue at the competing stations.

Kelly had thought his interviews on that subject had been particularly pompous, though she agreed completely with his judgment. The public had tired of anchormen who smiled vacantly through reports of car accidents, murders, and earthquakes with equal aplomb. On his newscasts the humor was left to the sportscaster and the weatherman.

As she mentally ticked off the professional information she'd read, Grant gazed down at her from his towering six-foot-two vantage point. She met the interested, speculative look in his eyes evenly.

"You know, Mr. Andrews, I'm looking forward to working with you," she said sincerely. "You've got quite a reputation in this business."

"Not all of it bad, I hope."

"Certainly not with regard to your work."

"What about the rest?" he taunted wickedly. "Do I have a reputation as a rogue all the way to Dallas?"

A quick image of those polls and several gossip-column items linking his name to a long string of beautiful women, from models to socialites, flashed through Kelly's mind. However, she was not about to be drawn into a discussion of the anchorman's morals.

"Your private life is none of my business, Mr. Andrews," she said firmly.

He gave her a long look, his gaze lingering on her eyes, which blazed back at him defiantly. "We could make it your business," he suggested lightly, "especially if you'd relax and call me Grant."

Instinctively, Kelly's guard went up. Long ago she had learned to protect herself from male colleagues who sought a greater intimacy than she was prepared to offer. She had become a master of sharp retorts calculated to silence such overtures. She was ready with one now, but, fortunately, she caught the devilish gleam in Grant's eyes and the hint of a smile tugging at the corners of his mouth.

"Why don't we stick with Mr. Andrews for the moment?" she said coolly. "It has a nice businesslike ring to it."

"Is that so I'll remember who's boss?" he inquired. Then, his tone lightly mocking, he added, "Or so you will?"

Kelly could not keep a blush from tinting her fair complexion a rosy pink. She tried to cover the plainly visible crack in her sophisticated veneer by stating sharply, "You're edging out of line, Mr. Andrews."

"Am I really?" He sounded doubtful. "How far?" he wondered aloud in a tone that was far from apologetic. He ran his fingers through his thick brown hair in an unconscious gesture that left it mussed and unruly, reminding Kelly once more of how natural and decidedly masculine he was compared to the perfectly groomed, flashy "pretty boys" anchoring most of the nation's newscasts. No, he was a newsman through and through, she could see. Not some glamor boy more concerned with being shot at his best angle than getting the facts straight.

Her composure slowly came back and her sense of humor along with it. She replied with a smile, "Far enough."

"I was only trying to live up to my reputation . . . as you see it," he said innocently. "I certainly wouldn't want to disappoint the new general manager."

"You'll disappoint me only if your ratings start to drop," she assured him. "As for your reputation, feel free to live up to that on your own time. I'm sure you have more than enough opportunities."

"More than enough," he agreed, his tone suddenly mocking, as though the thought of all those easy conquests the thought. . . was somehow distasteful. Before Kelly could analyze his reaction, he continued. "Just for the record, Miss Patrick, I'm on my own time now. The station pays me for my undivided attention from late afternoon until the end of the ten o'clock news Monday through Friday. This is Saturday and I'm off duty."

"Should I be grateful that you showed up?" Kelly asked, her eyes meeting his with a challenging look.

"Not especially. It was a command performance," he admitted with a smile that displayed his perfect, gleaming white teeth. Something about the unexpectedness and the boyish sincerity of that smile made Kelly's heart pound crazily in her chest.

"When Lyndon Phillips speaks, it's just like the stockbroker's ad says, I listen."

"Just because he's the boss?" she asked, her curiosity aroused.

"Because I respect him," he replied pointedly. "And, yes, to a certain extent, because he is the boss."

"Does that mean you'll listen to me?"

He gave her a slow, appraising look. "When it suits my purposes," he teased. Then he added more seriously, "You haven't been around long enough to earn my respect. Not the way Lyndon has."

"Is longevity all it will take?"

"Hardly."

"What then?" she asked, surprised to find herself so interested in his response. Normally she cared little about what others thought of her performance as long as she was pleased with it.

"I'll be watching to see how you handle yourself when the chips are really down. That's always the best test of a good man," he told her, amending himself quickly as she bristled, "or a good woman."

Years of hearing condescension in the voices of men who refused to take her seriously should have steeled her to that attitude, but she found she was still overly sensitive to every nuance. Now she retorted far too sharply to what she thought she heard in Grant's tone. "Don't expect me to fail the test, Mr. Andrews."

"Why would I expect that?" he countered, seemingly puzzled by her reaction. "After all, Lyndon did give you the job and I've already told you that I respect his judgment."

"Is that supposed to be a vote of confidence?" Kelly asked.

"Why? Do you need one from me?"

"Of course not," she snapped, irritated more with her own behavior than with Grant.

"I didn't think so. You don't strike me as a woman much in need of reassurance. Just the opposite, in fact. I've never met anyone more in control of herself."

"Are you always this quick to form impressions?" she asked, feeling somehow hurt by his observation. "I thought journalists were trained to be objective."

He grinned at her infuriatingly. "We are, except when a beautiful woman's involved. Then all sorts of things get in the way of our objectivity."

"In that case I hope you don't interview too many beautiful women for the station, Mr. Andrews. I'd hate to have you accused of biased reporting."

"I wasn't aware I was interviewing you, Miss Patrick," he responded easily. "But if it will make you feel any better, I'll promise to regard you only as a source in the future and I'll take my time assessing you."

"What happens if I don't live up to your high standards?" she asked. "Will you do an exposé on the evening news?"

He seemed to consider the idea seriously. "It's a thought, but I doubt if Lyndon would like it much.

He doesn't appreciate having his authority challenged in public."

"Perhaps you ought to remember that," she suggested, a certain defensiveness surfacing in her tone.

Refusing to be goaded by her attitude, Grant merely smiled and said, "Perhaps you ought to remember that your power is only as good as Lyndon Phillips makes it. Go against his wishes just once and you'll discover quickly that all the strings are being pulled down in Dallas—mine and, most especially, yours."

"Is that bitter personal experience talking?"

He paused, considering her question a moment. "Not personal, no. But in ten years I've seen a lot of people come and go," he said finally. "Some of them never realized that Lyndon's control over this whole operation is absolute. No one, not even you, golden girl, bucks his authority for long and survives."

"I'm surprised you've tolerated that," Kelly said. "You don't strike me as the type who'd allow anyone to run your life, not even a man you say you respect."

"Lyndon Phillips has never tried to run my life, Miss Patrick. That's one reason we've gotten along so well," he said slowly. Then, so swiftly that Kelly was taken aback, all remnants of their earlier bantering vanished. Grant's voice hardened perceptibly and his eyes became glittering bits of green glass. "Don't make the mistake of thinking you'll change that," he said coldly.

"That sounds like a threat, Mr. Andrews."

"Perhaps," he said, matching the coolness in her

voice. "On the other hand, perhaps it's only a warning."

"I don't like threats . . . or warnings," she advised him harshly, "especially not from someone who works for me."

He watched calmly as Kelly's anger mounted. "That can always change," he suggested, his tone mildly taunting.

"Yes. It certainly can," she lashed back before she could stop herself.

The outburst seemed only to amuse him. "Careful, Miss Patrick," he mocked. "Lyndon would hate it if you fired me even before your first day on the job."

With that, he slid his jacket from her shoulders, turned, and walked away without a backward glance, his lithe, athletic body moving with easy confidence. Kelly watched him go with a mixture of fury and, ironically, something approaching admiration. Although she was appalled by his gall and his blatant challenge of her authority, she found herself reluctantly approving of his brash self-assurance. It was a quality she could relate to, proving to her, if irritatingly so, that Grant Andrews was clearly his own man.

Before she'd had time to analyze her reaction more deeply, she heard Lyndon Phillips's booming voice approaching.

"Here's the little lady, gentlemen," he announced heartily to the two men he had in tow. They looked like children being forced to pay a duty call on a tiresome, grumpy old aunt. "Kelly dear, I thought for a minute you'd done slipped away from this shindig."

"You know I'd never walk out on one of your parties, Mr. Phillips, especially not when it's for me," she said smoothly, trying to focus her attention on the men before her. Her eyes, though, continued to follow the ramrod straight back of Grant Andrews as he made his way through the crowded living room.

Although Lyndon Phillips enjoyed capitalizing on his carefully perfected good-ole-boy image, as Grant had said earlier, he was a shrewd businessman and he watched Kelly now with undisguised interest. Following the direction of her gaze, he caught sight of the departing anchorman. Like a chess player who's just watched his opponent unwittingly move straight into his trap, he smiled benignly.

After only a few minutes of casual conversation between Kelly and the two salesmen to whom he'd just introduced her, the Texan dismissed them summarily and faced his companion.

"So, my dear, what did you think of our star attraction?"

Kelly sensed he was asking far more than the question actually implied. Injecting a cool, disinterested note into her voice, she replied, "I assume you mean Grant Andrews?"

"Who else?" he said, clearly amused by her pretense.

"I thought he was"—she hesitated before adding cautiously—"interesting."

"Got your back up, did he?" Mr. Phillips guessed astutely. Kelly grimaced at his perceptiveness. The man could see right through her.

"We didn't exactly embrace fondly and swear undying loyalty and support, if that's what you mean," she responded, thinking what an understatement that was. She thought she detected a hint of a smile flicker across Mr. Phillips's face at her words, but he was thoroughly serious when he chided her. "Just remember that he's a hot property, Kelly."

She tried not to look disgusted by the phrase. It reminded her all too graphically of how management in broadcasting tended to regard its on-air talent only as pawns in a game being played for exceptionally high stakes. They were rarely viewed as human beings or accorded much dignity. Mr. Phillips caught the expression on her face and accurately assessed its cause.

"I can see you think I'm nothing but a callous old businessman," he told her. "Kelly, you've had to make some tough decisions. Otherwise you wouldn't be where you are today. You know what I'm saying is the truth."

"I know it," she said wearily. "But I don't have to like it."

"No. You don't. But you do have to remember that Grant Andrews's contract is up at the end of this year and it's up to you to see that he renews it. We can't afford to lose the top anchorman in town. It took us a long time to achieve respectability in news here and he's the one who did it for us."

His deadly serious tone reminded her uneasily of Grant's lightly spoken parting shot. He had known that Lyndon Phillips would not tolerate her firing him. Nor would he tolerate any action she might take that would cause the anchorman to quit. It was beginning to appear that her own fate was inextricably bound up with Grant Andrews's future relationship with the station. Already sensing the response, she asked, "What if I can't keep him?"

"Then, my dear, you will have had the shortest career as head of a top television station of anyone in the industry," he replied coldly. There was not the slightest trace of humor behind the words, though Kelly listened desperately for some.

As though sensing that he might be pushing her too far, he added in a more kindly tone, "Of course, it's not going to come to that. I'm convinced you'll find a way to keep Mr. Andrews happy."

Every ounce of the professionalism in which Kelly took such pride was rankled by the implied order to use her feminine wiles, if need be, to appease the anchorman. Facing Mr. Phillips defiantly, she demanded, "Exactly what are you suggesting?"

"I'm telling you to see to it that Grant Andrews signs a new contract," he repeated simply, his voice washing over her like a smooth whiskey that leaves a trail of fire in its wake. He emphasized his point with burning intensity. "Any way you have to."

There was something in the way the Texan was regarding her that made Kelly suspect for the first time that she had been set up from the start.

"That's why you hired me, isn't it?" she accused him, almost laughing at the irony of it. "Because I'm a woman?"

"I hired you because I thought you were the best person for the job," he insisted.

"But exactly which of my qualifications made me the most suitable? My résumé or my looks?" she persisted.

Kelly knew she was attractive, though it had rarely mattered to her. She accepted with unquestioning ease the fact that men appreciated her tall, slim figure, the wavy blond mane that no amount of styling could control, the smooth, pale complexion, and the deep blue eyes.

She had never knowingly traded on her appearance to get a job. In fact, she had often gone to extremes to play down her femininity with tailored suits in businesslike navy, gray, or black, with plain pumps and simple blouses, with her thick hair secured in a neat, no-nonsense bun. Her only jewelry was a gold locket, inherited from her grandmother, and she wore it constantly, as though it were a good-luck charm.

If she had avoided flaunting her looks, she also had most certainly never slept with anyone to get or to keep a job. The thought that Lyndon Phillips had judged her on anything other than her professional merits infuriated her. The look she gave him now was devastating and filled with derision, but he seemed not the least bit intimidated by her obvious anger.

"The combination," he told her calmly. "It's a potent one, Kelly Patrick, and you might as well make the most of it. You add a little charm and a little style and you'll climb straight to the top. You're already a whole lot further along than most men your age. There's not a man here tonight who's not envious of your position."

"And probably not a one who doesn't wonder whether I got it by bouncing around in bed with the station owner," she muttered bitterly under her breath. Aloud, she said with conviction, "And I intend to prove to them that I deserved it because I'm damn good at what I do and not because you thought I might be able to provide an attractive piece of bait for Grant Andrews."

"Blast it all, woman, I know you're good. You don't think I'd jeopardize this station by turning it over to some empty-headed female? Not even to keep Grant. And you don't have to prove a thing to those people on staff. I'm the one who counts, and I'm one hundred percent in your corner."

Kelly's reply was laced with biting sarcasm. "If you don't mind my saying so, that's not terribly reassuring. You've already made it quite plain that I'll deliver Grant or I'll be in that corner all alone."

Lyndon Phillips's hearty laugh boomed out across the balcony, drifting away on the night air and leaving in its wake a decidedly uneasy atmosphere. Although he'd apparently found her acerbic comment amusing, his next words were cold.

"You've known for a long time what this business

is like. If you suddenly don't like the rules, perhaps you should get out."

As much as Kelly hated hearing it, she knew he was right. Television was a cutthroat business. The trade papers were littered with barbed items about the good guys who'd been trampled on by someone not necessarily brighter but clearly more ruthless. She had wanted to be different, to inject some sense of humanity into it all, but perhaps that wasn't possible. If it weren't, Lyndon was right: She would have to do some serious reevaluating of her goals. Tonight, though, was not the time and this was not the place. Reluctantly, she decided to let the matter drop for the moment.

"Okay," she said more calmly. "You've made your point. Now, why don't we go back inside and see if I can start mending some of those fences you tore down by bringing me here in the first place?"

Back in the living room, she left Lyndon Phillips's side and moved from group to group, ignoring the hush that accompanied her arrival and the subsequent coolness of her reception. She'd done her homework carefully to prepare for this evening though, and she was able to put the knowledge to good use, asking about children, family illnesses, a favorite sport. Her obvious interest in the replies, combined with her careful avoidance of anything having to do with the station or its politics, began a subtle thawing process she hoped would help her on Monday morning.

As she progressed through the room, her eyes

were constantly on the alert for Grant Andrews. Once she caught sight of him with a petite, sultry brunette, who was clinging possessively to his arm. He turned in Kelly's direction at just that instant and their eyes met and clashed in some unspecified challenge. An instant later he was gone. The brunette, however, remained, her presence after Grant's departure offering Kelly a welcome and, therefore, disquieting sense of relief.

Later, back in her hotel suite, she tried to reflect calmly and rationally on each of the evening's encounters. Her shoes off and her feet tucked under her as she sat curled up in a corner of the sofa, she allowed herself the luxury of unwinding from the night's multileveled tensions. Although her intention, as she sipped slowly from a small snifter of brandy, was to consider the progress she had made with the staff, it was the anchorman's image that remained firmly implanted in the forefront of her mind.

Although certain of his remarks continued to irritate her, she was even more infuriated with herself for losing control and lashing back at him angrily. In retrospect, even his harshest comments had been relatively mild barbs compared to many she had fended off during her career. Why had she reacted so unprofessionally when faced with Grant's taunts?

The answer was obvious, though she hated to admit it. The man evoked a very feminine response in her, an immediate and undeniable awareness of his virility and strength. The suddenness of its impact and its depth startled and frightened her. For years now she had been playing it safe, seeking companionship with men who posed no threat to her independence. Such uncomplicated relationships had allowed her to devote her total energies to her career. And, after struggling to put herself through school, to be better than the rest so that each new goal would be quickly attained, broadcasting had been her primary lover and companion.

Nor, to be perfectly honest, had there ever been anyone exciting enough to seriously challenge her dedication to her profession. The few men who might have interested her were quickly put off by her success. They viewed her as a competitor rather than as a woman. They courted her as they would court any bright, attractive female, but they also seemed to fear her and, so, even those few potentially rewarding relationships had foundered. Burned once or twice in this way, she had no desire to repeat such emotional masochism.

Now here was Grant Andrews, a man capable of threatening not only her emotional serenity, but her career as well. Every instinct in her warned her to stay as far away from him as possible. Ironically, though, Lyndon Phillips had made that impossible. He had virtually dared her to see this through, to prove she was tough enough for the business. And, by God, she was going to prove that she was.

No one, least of all Grant himself, need ever know about her fears, the panic she felt in his presence. If she could draw on her professionalism during their meetings, she would be able to hide this unwanted attraction he seemed to hold for her. Her professionalism, she realized as she sighed deeply, was the only protective cloak she had. She could only pray it would be sufficient.

CHAPTER TWO

Kelly sat in her office at ten o'clock Monday morning facing a roomful of hostile stares. Whatever slim hope she had had that Saturday night would smooth the way for this first staff meeting had vanished this morning, along with her patience.

She had arrived at the station at eight thirty A.M., expecting to call in the top management people within the next half-hour, only to discover that no one else was around in the executive suite, including her own secretary. She had paced the room angrily, oblivious to its expensive, tasteful furnishings, until nine o'clock, when a surprised Janie Wilkins had stuck her head in the door. The pert redhead, whom Kelly had met on previous visits to the station, gaped at her new boss in amazement.

"You're here already," she'd said, her expression thunderstruck. "Mr. Randall never came in before ten."

"Apparently he wasn't the only one," Kelly observed wryly. "Tell me, Janie, what time can I expect the rest of the staff?"

"They should be in shortly," she'd answered vaguely.

Kelly hid a smile at the girl's protectiveness. "What time?" she repeated.

"They're usually in by nine thirty or ten at the latest," Janie conceded reluctantly.

"Okay. Would you see if you can round everyone up and have them in here promptly at ten?"

"Certainly, Miss Patrick," the girl said eagerly, rushing from the room.

Apparently Janie had accomplished her assignment with an unusually authoritative style, because the expressions of the men and women now seated around the room ranged from mild annoyance to outright resentment. Kelly suspected that for the moment the attitude was based on this morning's abrupt change in their normal work habits rather than her presence at the station in the first place. She decided, though, that she'd better face both issues squarely from the outset. Otherwise today's pattern was more than likely to repeat itself.

"Good morning," she began, her voice firm despite the nervous flutter in her stomach.

Maintaining a psychological advantage by remaining behind her desk, she continued smoothly. "I want very much for all of us to get along. I know that many of you had expected to be in this office yourselves or hoped that one of your friends would be. And, I'm equally sure, none of you expected to find a woman in here." She smiled slightly. "I must admit I'm a little surprised myself."

There was a scattering of uneasy laughter, and several of the men shifted uncomfortably in their chairs.

"However, most of you know Lyndon Phillips. He's a man who does what he pleases, no matter what the rest of the world thinks of his decisions," Kelly said, returning to a matter-of-fact tone. "We could spend a lot of time trying to second-guess my presence here, but it would be a wasted effort. The decision is out of our hands. I honestly hope that I can gain your respect and your confidence. In the meantime, however, I must demand your cooperation. If any of you feel that you are incapable of working with me, please say so now. Running this station will be enough of a challenge without my having to fight internal battles along with battling our competition."

Kelly glanced around the room and noticed that a few of the men were exchanging skeptical looks. Directing her gaze at them, she asked pointedly, "Anyone leaving?" She allowed the question to hang in the air for several minutes, knowing that with each moment's delay in breaking the silence tension was mounting.

When no one accepted her challenge, she nodded in satisfaction. "Good. Once these first awkward days are over, I'm sure we'll be able to build a solid team. You are all experts in your respective areas, and I'll be relying on you a great deal over the next few weeks."

The tension eased slightly with this subtle bit of

flattery and Kelly promptly strengthened her position by adding, "I will be arranging meetings with each of you over the next few days to discuss your particular department. I've been reading your reports for the last month, but I'd like you to be prepared to expand on the information they contained. I'll also want to hear any ideas you have about improvements we need to make. Then we can begin planning for the future."

They nodded at her words and, for the first time, many of them regarded her with something approaching respect. When she dismissed them, there were polite comments and enthusiastic murmurings as they headed for the door. Before the first of them had exited, Kelly stopped them.

"One last thing," she said distinctly, moving around to stand in front of her desk, "I arrive here by nine at the latest. I feel it's helpful to be on approximately the same work schedule as the networks in New York, despite the time difference. I would appreciate it if you would all be here at that time as well. I may need your input on a decision that needs to be made quickly."

Her announcement was greeted by a moment of shocked silence, followed by reluctant nods of agreement. As the last of the group neared the door, Kelly called him back.

"John, could you wait a minute, please? There's something you and I need to discuss right away."

"Sure, Miss Patrick," the gray-haired man said easily, returning to a seat by her desk. Of all of the executives in the room, only John Marshall had seemed totally comfortable during the brief meeting. At times, in fact, he'd seemed downright amused, though he'd tried hard to cover it. He knew that a lot of egos had been shattered during that session, despite the superficial politeness. Some of those egos should have been deflated years ago, but Ted Randall had never had the stomach for confrontations. As long as the station had remained on firm financial ground, he'd been content. Kelly had made it clear this morning that things were about to change.

Now she closed the door before returning to perch on the arm of the chair next to Marshall. Only he would have noticed the signs of strain behind her bravely spoken words. "I thought it went fairly well, didn't you?"

John grinned at her. "I'd say old man Phillips would have been proud of you. He brought you in here to kick ass and that's exactly what you did. Of course, you're not likely to win any popularity contests around here for a while."

Kelly returned his smile. "I didn't come here to become elected Miss Congeniality. I came here to run a television station."

"In that case, you're on your way. These guys will come around if you're firm with them. At least most of them will. As for the one or two who don't, well, they won't be a big loss. The place has a lot of dead wood, most of it at the top."

Kelly regarded the older man fondly. "I'm glad

you're here, John. It was nice to find at least one friendly face in the crowd."

"Always glad to oblige an old friend," he replied. "Just don't go cutting my news budget on me."

She chuckled at the lightly spoken warning. She and John Marshall had worked together in Dallas when she had just started her climb up at the station. John had been news director for a number of years and he'd taken her under his wing and encouraged her to aim for the top. She could see that he was proud of her accomplishments, but she wondered a little if he harbored any resentment about suddenly finding himself working for her. She decided to approach the issue head-on.

"John, did you want this job?"

"What?" he said, his expression stunned.

"Well, you are the senior man in the Phillips organization. It wouldn't be illogical to assume you'd be first in line for general manager here."

He smiled at the serious look on her face as she regarded him closely. "Kelly, I'm a newsman—first, last, and always. All I want out of life is to put together the best newscast money can buy, to see to it that the public is informed about the issues that affect them. Programing, advertisers, ratings, financial reports"—he gave his head a shake—"lady, you're *welcome* to all of that. Just let me keep chasing firetrucks and crooked politicians."

Kelly nodded, satisfied with his answer. "I thought that was the way you felt, but I had to be sure."

"I appreciate your concern," he said sincerely. Then, after studying her for several minutes, he added, "That's not the only thing on your mind though, is it?"

She shook her head. "I want to know how much trouble we're likely to have getting Grant Andrews to sign his new contract."

John Marshall was the man who'd made the decision to put Grant on the air as an anchorman and, Kelly had heard, the two had become good friends. She needed every bit of insight John Marshall could give her into Grant's personality.

"The old man got you nervous?"

Kelly nodded. "That's an understatement. It seems I'd be wise not to unpack until Andrews is signed, sealed, and delivered."

John whistled softly. "He laid it on the line that plainly?"

"I get our star anchor to stick around for another three years or I'll be out of here before he is," she said shortly.

"Well, I'll tell you what I think, Kelly. I'm fairly certain that Grant wants to stay in Chicago. He's had network offers, some of them as recently as last month. He's turned them all down."

"Why?" Kelly couldn't conceal her surprise. She would have guessed that no man in Grant's position would turn down a chance at national recognition.

"I'm not sure," John said slowly. "He seems to have found something here that's important to him."

"Okay. So he wants to stay in Chicago for some

reason. But what about this station? Does he want to stay here?"

"My guess is that he does, but I wouldn't rely heavily on that when you're negotiating with him," John suggested, reminding Kelly of Grant's warning on Saturday night. "Grant is stubborn, maybe even a little arrogant, but he's also a damn good journalist. He knows he can go to any other station in town. I don't think he'll do it unless he's backed into a corner and has no other choice. My advice is that you try like hell not to back him into one."

"Is he after money?"

"No more than anyone else in his position. Oddly enough, I think he's more concerned with respect and stability. We've given him both in the past . . . along with a hefty salary and benefits package."

"So you think I should appeal to his ego rather than his greed." She was not even looking at John now, her lips pursed in concentration, her mind already churning away at the problem.

"Something like that. You arranged deals all the time in Dallas. Handling Grant Andrews is no different."

"A thick steak, a bottle of wine, and a lot of sweet talk about how important he is to the station?"

"That's the idea."

The vision of an intimate little tête-à-tête with Grant made Kelly more than a little uneasy. But she couldn't let John Marshall know that. She grimaced as she recalled the terms on which she and the anchorman had parted on Saturday night.

"Looks as though I'll be eating crow instead of steak," she admitted.

"Why?"

"Grant Andrews and I didn't exactly hit it off at the party the other night. If I'm going to wine-and-dine him, I'll have to get him to speak to me first."

John groaned. "What happened to everything I taught you about professional diplomacy?"

"I remembered every word . . . after he'd walked off in a huff. Don't panic though. I remember how to smooth things over."

"Good, because you're going to have to. If you and Grant can't negotiate a contract on your own, you'll be left to deal with his agent, a guy who makes Lyndon Phillips look like a doddering old fool. He's tough and sharp and he'll force you to promise half this station to Grant and make you believe it was all your own idea. Just see how our boss down in Dallas likes those terms when you have to explain them to him."

"God forbid!" Kelly said fervently. "Okay, pal. Thanks for your help."

"Anytime," he said, "Just remember, I'm betting on you."

"In that case, how can I lose? Now, get out of here and go run your news department. And don't go over your budget. I may need every penny we've got in reserve to keep your anchorman for you."

When John Marshall had gone, Kelly sank down in the highbacked executive chair behind her massive mahogany desk and considered the problem ahead of her. "Make it or break it, Patrick," she muttered to herself, the thought making her pulse race a beat faster. Anxious to plan a strategy, she buzzed for Janie.

"Bring me all our files on Grant Andrews," she told her, "and call the legal department and have them send in his contracts."

Janie had the requested material on her desk within ten minutes and Kelly spent the rest of the morning going through it. Most of the clippings she had already read, but the contracts were new to her. She studied them closely, and as she made notes on the terms, she realized how accurate John's assessment had been. Grant's salary increases had been substantial, but there were dozens of seemingly insignificant clauses about fringe benefits indicating how important the extras were to him.

With an order of tuna fish and a cup of coffee sitting virtually untouched on her desk, she worked through lunch planning her strategy, determining what she could offer Grant to make him stay. She settled on a salary range she knew Lyndon Phillips would accept and a benefits package that seemed reasonable. The only thing left, then, was to sell it to the anchorman.

Taking a deep breath, she asked Janie to get him on the phone for her. Tapping her pen nervously on her desk, she waited for the call to come through. It seemed to happen all too quickly.

"Miss Patrick, Mr. Andrews is on line one," Janie announced, her voice evidence that she was as much in awe of the anchorman as the rest of Chicago's female population.

"Thanks, Janie," she said, hesitating only a moment before picking up the line. "Mr. Andrews, how are you?"

"Just fine, boss. How's the first day on the job?"

"Educational," she admitted cautiously. "I'm still trying to get all the names straight. Except for yours, of course. It seems to pop up in almost every conversation."

"Oh?" he said, a note of feigned innocence in his voice. "Why is that? Is everyone telling you what a great guy I am?"

"Not exactly. They've been reminding me that your contract is up in a few months. I think we should get together and start talking about a new one."

"Fine," he said agreeably. Then, apparently unable to resist an opportunity to provoke her, he added suggestively, "Your place or mine?"

"Unless you were referring to offices, I think we've got a bad connection," she responded tartly.

He sighed heavily. "Well, you can't blame me for trying, golden girl."

"I suppose not," she conceded. "But I could always knock off a few dollars when we start the negotiating." She smiled to herself as she heard his sharp intake of breath. "Don't worry, Mr. Andrews, you haven't blown the deal—yet."

"In that case, let's talk soon before I say something that will really antagonize you."

"I can't imagine your doing that," Kelly said sweetly, "but how about tonight? Just to be safe, of course."

"Of course," he mocked. "Over dinner?"

"Why not?" Kelly agreed. "You'll pick the place?"

"Sure. I'll come by your office right after the early news and we can go someplace close by so I can get back here in time for the ten o'clock show."

"That sounds perfect, Mr. Andrews. I'll be looking forward to it."

"So will I, Miss Patrick, so will I," he said, his voice provocatively low. Then in a more businesslike tone he added, "While you're waiting, why don't you tune in the show? It might give you a few ideas about what we can discuss over dinner."

"Oh, I'll be watching," she assured him. "Of course, I've already seen your tapes. You don't have to convince me that you're quite good on the air."

"Then I'll just have to demonstrate how good I am off the air, as well," he teased her. Kelly sensed he knew exactly how his little innuendos threw her. The man was impossible, she thought, wondering anew at his ability to maneuver her.

Determined to turn the tables on him, though, she asked briskly, "Are you suggesting we make your personal behavior a part of this new contract?"

He laughed. "Touché. I'm beginning to see why Lyndon hired you," he said admiringly. "You have a sharp tongue, lady. Just be careful it doesn't get you into trouble one of these days."

Before she could respond, he had hung up and she was left holding a dead phone. She stared at it as though Grant were somewhere inside. "Damn the man," she muttered, slamming it back into place at last.

It was becoming more and more evident that three performances in *Our Town* in high school and a walk-on role in *Macbeth* in college had not exactly prepared her for the acting assignment called for in this new job. She hadn't bargained for playing the role of a sophisticated, witty seductress and, yet, this was obviously what was called for. And, she realized with a growing sense of dismay, if she didn't learn her lines by tonight, Grant Andrews was going to steal the whole show.

CHAPTER THREE

There were three color television monitors built into a wall console in Kelly's office, and each was tuned to a different channel during the early newscasts. Although she had viewed repeatedly a selection of sample tapes from her own station, this was the first opportunity she had had to see how those shows stacked up against the competition. More familiar with comparing the relative merits of syndicated game shows, she was finding this to be a fascinating exercise. It troubled her, however, that she was having difficulty concentrating on the competition with Grant's gaze seemingly directed straight at her as he briskly introduced the day's top stories. All too often she found herself bemusedly returning that gaze, the notes in her lap forgotten along with the other newscasts.

While she awaited Grant's arrival, she tried to force herself to be more analytical about what she had observed. Clearly the chemistry of the people on the air with Grant was superb. Grant himself was like a skilled conductor pulling each of the diverse instruments in an orchestral arrangement into a musical whole. Although John Marshall and his directors might have staged and choreographed the telecast, once it was in the hands of the anchorman it was his to conduct, and he did it magnificently.

Not only did he work well with each of the reporters brought onto the set to do live lead-ins to their own stories, but he had a natural rapport with the sportscaster and weatherman. Kelly found herself feeling almost envious of that easygoing camaraderie. The people on this newscast actually appeared to enjoy working together, and that enjoyment was conveyed to the viewer without any loss of dignity.

But as important as Grant's ability to share the limelight with his colleagues was his uncanny knack for working with the camera. He treated that gaping eye, which Kelly had always found thoroughly intimidating, as though it were his best friend and he was merely sharing the news with him. But, instead of talking over the days' events with a single, intelligent companion, Grant was reaching thousands of viewers at once, bringing them an abundance of information from around the world in concise, easy-to-understand reports.

Kelly was still lost in thought, admiring his exceptional skill, when there was a light tap on her door and Grant poked his head in.

"Ready, boss lady?" he inquired lightly, stepping into the office and surveying her closely from across the room. "By the way, the desk suits you. You look perfectly at home."

"Thanks," she said, adding dryly, "though after what you said the other night, perhaps I shouldn't get too comfortable." It was the closest she could come to bringing up the sour note on which their conversation had ended at the party. Grant, thank goodness, actually laughed at the remark.

"I imagine you'll have time to bring in a few plants and personal items, family photographs, that sort of thing," he replied.

"But I should keep a packing carton in the closet?"

"Perhaps," he agreed, a dazzling smile taking the edge from his comment. Kelly returned the smile and, for a moment, she forgot all about the role she was supposed to be playing and simply responded to his teasing and the warm look in his eyes as they raked over her body with masculine appreciation.

Falling easily into step with his mood, she told him sincerely, "By the way, you did a terrific job tonight. The other stations had essentially the same stories, but there was something . . . I don't know . . . special about the way you held it all together."

"Don't give me the credit for that," he said humbly. "If the show goes smoothly, the credit goes to John and the guys in the booth, not me. They're the best in the business."

Kelly was impressed by his unassuming display of modesty. Perhaps Grant Andrews wasn't like all the other shallow media celebrities with whom she had dealt. Certainly John Marshall didn't seem to think he was and John's judgment about character was usually impeccable. The thought intrigued and frightened her. She might be able to pull off her assigned role with little personal damage if she had only to play to the anchorman's conceit. However, if depth and intelligence were there instead, along with the virility that stoked her senses to a level of fiery awareness, she was treading on far more dangerous ground.

There was no time to ponder this latest development though, for Grant was beckoning to her. "Let's get out of here," he suggested. "I want the rest of our conversation to take place on neutral turf."

"Don't tell me you're intimidated by this office?" she taunted as she joined him.

"Only what it represents," he retorted.

"Which is?"

"Power, to put it bluntly. Possibly only limited, but power nonetheless."

Kelly gazed up and saw the twinkle in his eye. "And you can't bear the thought of a woman having power over you?"

"I don't want *anyone* to get the idea they have power over me. You may be drawing up the contract, sweetheart, but I'm the one who'll decide whether to sign. Call it a balance of power if you will."

"Ah, but right now that balance is tipped in my favor," she replied confidently.

"Is it really?" he asked softly, linking her arm through his as they walked to the elevator.

Kelly tried to pretend that the contact with his hard, muscular arm was no different from that of any other male business associate, but the rapid beating of her pulse told her otherwise. Forcing herself to sound far more casual than she felt, she asked, "Where are we going for dinner?"

"I made a reservation at the Pump Room at the Ambassador," he told her as they rode to the ground floor of the skyscraper.

Kelly whistled softly. "Expensive taste," she noted.

"Why not?" he replied with a grin. "Especially since you're buying."

"I am?"

"Of course. It's all part of your campaign to woo me into staying with the station."

"That's odd," Kelly said, a note of puzzlement in her voice. "I thought we were having dinner so you could convince me I should keep you."

"Lady, you already know you want to keep me," he said with smug self-assurance. "The only thing left to work out is the price."

"If that's the case, why are we bothering with dinner? We could go over that minor little detail in my office." Her stress on the word *minor* bore a trace of sarcasm, which was not lost on her companion.

"Because I like to have a beautiful woman take me out every now and then. It's good for my ego."

"I suspect your ego doesn't need any help from me," she replied with a light laugh.

For several seemingly interminable seconds silence hung in the air between them until, at last, he said quite seriously, "You might be surprised about that, boss lady."

He turned away then to stare moodily out the window as the taxi crept through the rush-hour traffic toward the Ambassador. What a bundle of contradictions this man was turning out to be, Kelly thought to herself as she regarded him closely. On the one hand, Grant seemed totally at ease, a man comfortable with himself and his niche in the world. And, yet, she had to admit there had been the merest shadow of uncertainty in his eyes as he had revealed a vulnerability most men would fight to conceal.

Turning back to her at last, he asked, "What are you thinking about?"

She hesitated only an instant before confessing. "I was just reminding myself that things—and people—are not always what they seem to be on the surface."

"*People* rarely are," he corrected her. "We've developed into a generation of con artists, at least where our emotions are concerned. For instance, when was the last time you really told someone the whole truth about what you were thinking and feeling?"

"Telling the whole, unvarnished truth is not always for the best," she argued.

"Anything else is a lie," he stated flatly. "Nobody wins once the lying starts."

"Possibly not, but I've seen an awful lot of people inflict pain on one another in the guise of being honest."

"Is it any less painful to learn the truth later and

discover you've been living a lie for months, perhaps even years?"

"No," she admitted softly, thinking of her own belated awakening to the reality of a disastrously bad romance years earlier. Considering those agonizing months anew, she realized the role they'd played in driving her toward a career that would absorb all of her energy, in keeping her away from men who might reach out and touch the sensitive inner core of her being.

She was thankful when her soul-searching was brought to an end by the taxi's arrival at the hotel. Once they were inside the restaurant she felt her confidence returning. There had been something entirely too intimate about being alone with Grant, even in the back of a cab. In the Pump Room, with its muted decor and walls lined with celebrity photos, perhaps she could more safely play the role of seductress.

Kelly noticed the murmurs of recognition that spread through the room on their arrival. It was also obvious that the staff, from the maître d' to the busboys, knew Grant well and regarded him as a very special patron. They were taken to a secluded table, promptly served a bottle of perfectly chilled, expensive wine, and then left discreetly alone.

"Is this place known for its personalized service or are you the only one who rates?" Kelly inquired when the bowing maître d' had departed.

"Are you complaining?" Grant asked. "I'd have

thought you'd be delighted to know that your anchorman commands this sort of attention."

"I don't know. It might have improved my bargaining position if no one in the place had recognized you," she suggested flippantly, trying to divert him, and herself, from the real reason she had found the attention so disconcerting. An analysis would have told her that what had really bothered her were the openly interested stares of several very attractive women. Grant had nodded at more than one of them, bestowing on them that funny little half smile, that teasing wink that made her own pulse beat erratically.

Without pausing to consider her motive, Kelly suddenly found she wanted to do something to hold his attention. Placing her hand on his, she asked in what she hoped was a seductively low voice, "What made you come to Chicago, Grant?"

His eyes drifted from the hand she had allowed to linger on his to her lips and then on to meet her own by now unsteady gaze. From the way her heart was pounding in her chest, Kelly felt as though she had been thoroughly kissed, though Grant's body hadn't swayed even slightly in her direction. She sensed an underlying amusement in the way he was studying her, but when he spoke his response was serious enough.

"Who wouldn't want to come to Chicago? Especially if you're a small-town boy from Nebraska who's dreamed all his life of making it to the big city someday. Omaha, though a dozen times bigger than the place I grew up, is not a big city, but it was the biggest I'd ever seen."

"But why not New York? Or Los Angeles?"

"You might as well ask why not the moon? When you're just starting out, those places seem too far from reach. Chicago seemed attainable."

"And you only go after what's attainable?" Kelly asked.

"I did then," he said softly, accompanying the words with a look that nearly took Kelly's breath away. "Now I'm not so sure."

One part of Kelly wanted that caressing gaze to last forever, but her traditional caution forced her to retreat from it and all it implied. She tried to steer the conversation onto safer, less personal ground.

"Tell me what it was like growing up in Nebraska," she suggested, genuinely interested in learning more about this complex man. Suddenly what had begun as a game was taking an unexpected twist. No longer were her motives limited to prying from Grant information that might aid in her negotiations with him. She really wanted to understand him.

Throughout dinner he regaled her with stories of his boyhood, of the neighborhood paper he'd photocopied and sold for a nickel a copy until an irate friend of his parents had forced a halt to it.

"But why would he care about something like that? Sounds to me like you were just being an awfully enterprising kid."

"Oh, I was enterprising all right. I did my first investigative story on what a nice lady the mayor's wife must be since she dropped by every day to fix lunch for our neighbor. Our neighbor, his wife, and the mayor didn't find the story at all amusing," he told her, chuckling at the memory.

"I can imagine," Kelly said, joining in his laughter. "What did your parents say?"

"Well," he began conspiratorially, "I actually think they thought it was all pretty funny. They thought the mayor was a pompous old windbag. But they made me shut down my paper just the same."

"I'm surprised you didn't make a public protest about censorship of the press."

"I would have, if I'd known what it was. Instead, I decided to concentrate on playing basketball. It seemed less likely to offend any of the adults in town."

"Your parents must have been relieved," she suggested.

"Believe me, they were."

"But you never got over wanting to dig around and find out why things happen, did you?"

"Never. I love what I do, Miss Patrick," he said candidly.

"I know," she said, looking down at her wineglass for a moment. "I can see it in your eyes. There's an excitement there whenever you talk about your job. That's a wonderful thing. I feel the same way about mine. It's always seemed sad to me that so many people go through life without ever feeling that way about what they do." She was thinking of her own father and how much he'd hated the humdrum life of selling insurance day after day.

The waiter brought their coffee and, as they sat drinking it slowly, Kelly returned to a topic she had approached earlier. "I still don't understand something, Mr. Andrews. You're good. You've had network offers. John's told me about them. Why have you turned them down?"

"Because Chicago still suits my style," he replied cryptically, his suddenly curt tone suggesting that she put an end to this line of questioning. Again a closed look came over his face. Clearly he did not like being pressed about his desire to remain in Chicago when far bigger markets beckoned, but somehow Kelly couldn't make herself back off. She wanted to understand what motivated this man.

"What do you mean, it suits your style?"

Although the conversation up until now had seemed to be bringing them closer, now Grant seemed to visibly withdraw in the face of her persistence. "What possible difference could it make, Miss Patrick?" he asked coolly. "Unless, of course, you plan to use my desire to remain here to pressure me into signing a contract that's to your advantage."

Kelly was thrown by the swiftness of his attack and by the absolute unfairness of his charge. But, before she could counter it, he continued bitterly. "Another three-year deal. That's all that's important to you, isn't it? That's what all the charming manners and polite chit-chat are about. Right?"

His eyes were cold as he sat staring at her impassively, waiting for her response.

Stunned, she tried to bring her kaleidoscope of feelings into focus. To be sure, this had begun as a business meeting. Neither of them had made any pretense that it was otherwise. However, exploring the way her own feelings had changed over the last couple of hours in his company, she wondered if perhaps he too had fallen under the spell of the evening, allowing it, for the briefest of moments, to seem to be something else entirely. That might explain the look of icy disdain she now saw on his face, the anger and bitterness she had heard in his voice.

But, try as she might, she could think of no way to prove to him that his contract with Phillips Broadcasting had been the last thing on her mind while they had talked. Stiffly, she told him, "I'm sorry if you find it offensive or suspicious that I've been trying to get to know you better. From now on we'll limit our conversations strictly to business."

"I think that might be a good idea," he agreed, then waited patiently for her to speak. When she didn't, he said, "So, Miss Patrick, what's your offer?"

Kelly had been prepared for the question, though not for the skeptical, slightly sarcastic tone in which it was asked. Taking a deep breath, she said, "I'm prepared to increase your salary by ten thousand a year over the next three years. You'll continue to have a car and driver at your disposal. Your on-camera wardrobe will be furnished by the station. You'll have one month of vacation, plus three-day weekends once a month except during rating periods. And you'll be guaranteed three major investigative pieces a year, assignment to any major national stories covered by the station, and one overseas assignment a year."

She watched him carefully for his reaction, noting that he seemed momentarily taken aback by the speed and thoroughness of her response. But he recovered quickly.

"Not bad, Miss Patrick," he said, nodding his head in approval. "That's a very tempting offer."

"I think it's fair, based on the terms of your current contract. I don't think Lyndon will have any problem with it."

"Then you haven't discussed it with him?"

"No. He gave me the authority to handle the negotiations."

"It's probably just as well that he doesn't know about this."

"Why?"

"Because," he said simply, "I'm turning you down."

"You're what?" Kelly's voice climbed until she was practically shouting. Sensing the suddenly interested glances being cast in their direction, she lowered it. "What do you mean, you're turning it down? There's not another anchorman in Chicago with a deal that comes close to this. In fact, I doubt you could do better at a network."

"I probably couldn't," he agreed calmly.

Kelly had been prepared for an initial refusal, for

a counter-proposal, but she had not foreseen the finality with which Grant seemed to be turning down her offer. She tried to cover her dismay.

"Exactly what more do you expect to get from Phillips Broadcasting?" she asked.

Grant was finding her undisguised confusion amusing. The corners of his mouth tilted in an infuriating grin. "There's very little I want from the company," he told her tauntingly.

Kelly was baffled. "Then I don't understand. What is it you do want?"

"You, Miss Patrick," he said flatly. "I want you."

"You . . . you can't be serious," she said softly, expecting to hear a laughing denial.

Instead, he told her, "I've never been more serious in my life."

"But that's preposterous," she exploded somewhere between anger and incredulous laughter. "If you're that desperate for a bed partner, Mr. Andrews, I'm sure there are plenty of women in this room who would be only too happy to accommodate you. Just look around and take your pick. I'm leaving!"

She threw her napkin on the table and jumped up, knocking over her glass of ice water in her haste. As she stormed from the restaurant, she was only sorry the mess hadn't landed in his lap.

CHAPTER FOUR

Kelly slammed the door to her hotel suite behind her, still trying to vent her fury over Grant's arrogant assumption that she could be bought as part of his package with Phillips Broadcasting. How dare the man believe she would stoop that low! He didn't even know her and yet he seemed so sure of himself, so certain that all he had to do was quietly insist and she would fall willingly straight into his bed.

Well, she thought angrily, he could just go straight to hell and take Lyndon Phillips with him! That blasted Texan was the one who'd gotten her into this untenable situation in the first place. No, she admitted reluctantly as she began to calm down. Lyndon Phillips wasn't entirely to blame. She'd gotten herself into it. She was ambitious and she had wanted to believe she was ready and qualified to tackle a job of this size.

And, on the face of it, she was. She had been a quick study, paying her dues on the way up and absorbing every detail of the business from the brightest men and women around her. She had assumed that Lyndon Phillips had recognized her astuteness and rewarded her for it. Instead, she now knew he was the truly perceptive one. He had apparently sensed she would appeal to Grant Andrews and had thrown her to him, just as another attractive fringe benefit to ice the cake. No doubt he'd be pleased to know that Grant had made a grab for the bait.

The thought of how neatly she'd been caught up in this absurd situation only increased her rage and she stormed through the suite, tossing her purse in the direction of the sofa and managing, instead, to hit a small vase. She watched in horror as it shattered on the floor. Mechanically, she stooped to pick up the pieces, unaware of the tears that rolled down her cheeks.

"What a mess!" she murmured, not even sure whether she was referring to the vase or her life, which seemed to be breaking into similar tiny pieces.

When she'd cleaned up the bits of porcelain, she went into the bedroom, removed her clothes, and tossed them on the bed, then went into the bathroom and climbed into a hot shower, hoping that the steamy spray would relax the knotted muscles in her shoulders. As the water worked its magic and relieved at least some of the physical evidence of her tension, Kelly made a solemn oath that she would find a way out of this situation, a way to keep Grant at the station and in his place at the same time. She would prove to him and to Lyndon Phillips that they'd underestimated her.

The vow made, she briskly toweled herself dry until her skin shone with a healthy pink glow. She pulled on a loose caftan in shades of rose and mauve that flattered her coloring. Her hair, combed loose and damp from the shower, curled about her face even more haphazardly than usual. The entire effect was casual and, though she'd hardly intended it, decidedly sensual. It was a look that any man, but most especially a man like Grant, would find difficult, if not impossible, to resist. Irritated with herself, she banished the thought from her mind.

The image of Grant himself, however, would not flee quite so easily. As though drawn by some irresistible force, she went back into the suite's living room and switched on the television set just in time to catch a quick glimpse of him before he turned the show over to the sportscaster. He appeared as cool and self-possessed as ever. Obviously her reaction to his outrageous demand hadn't rattled him one bit or else he was a master at covering his own emotions.

When the news had ended, replaced by a Fred Astaire and Ginger Rogers movie, she didn't bother to turn the set off, though she paid little attention to the sound and movement on the screen. Instead, her mind ran over every word Grant had said to her at the restaurant, the tone of his voice that had switched from warm and sincere to coldly detached as he'd smoothly told her that she was the only thing that would keep him at the station.

She was still lost in thought when there was a firm knock at the door. "Who on earth?" she wondered aloud, knowing it must be well after eleven o'clock by now.

At the door she called out softly, "Who is it?"

"It's Grant. May I come in for a minute?"

Kelly gasped. The audacity of the man apparently knew no bounds. "No," she hissed angrily, taking a step backward.

"Please. I won't stay long," he promised. "I'd just like to straighten out a few things."

"I think you've already made your position quite clear, Mr. Andrews," Kelly retorted. "And I've told you what I've thought of it. I am not on the bargaining table."

"So I gathered," he said, and, to Kelly's absolute amazement, there was a note of amusement in his voice. He was incredible! He actually thought the entire episode was funny.

"Miss Patrick, you might as well let me in," he urged insistently. "I'm prepared to wait out here until you leave for work in the morning if I have to."

For a moment she was tempted to test him and leave him out there, but the idea of word about such an incident getting around town finally forced her to reconsider and open the door.

Staring at him defiantly, she said curtly, "All right, Mr. Andrews, your bullying tactics win this time, but keep it short. I'm in no mood for much more from you tonight."

He'd been leaning casually against the doorframe, his jacket off, his tie loosened, and his collar open. He held one arm behind him. As he straightened to accept her grudging invitation to come inside, he brought a bouquet of flowers from behind his back and held them out to her.

"A peace offering," he explained when she made no move to take the flowers. Finally, reluctantly, she accepted them.

"Thanks," she said grudgingly. "I'll find something to put them in." Relieved to have something to do to postpone the conversation a bit longer, she turned away, a trace of a smile on her lips at the thought of the broken vase in the wastebasket. Grant caught the look.

"Does the smile mean I'm forgiven?"

She faced him briefly with a scathing look. "Hardly," she retorted, quickly leaving the room in search of another vase.

When she returned, she found he had fixed himself a drink and was stretched out contentedly on the sofa. She wondered anew at his ability to dominate any situation. Even now, after all he'd said and done tonight, he was the one who was totally at ease, and in her living room at that! Her earlier anger began to return and she sat across from him, her stomach muscles feeling like a coiled spring as she waited for him to say something. If he'd come to apologize, he wasn't going to get any help from her, she thought stubbornly.

"About tonight," he said at last. "I think you may have jumped to the wrong conclusion."

"Oh?" she said suspiciously. "It seems to me there could be only one interpretation."

"There might have been another one if you'd allowed me to finish instead of rushing out of the restaurant in an indignant rage."

"Are you denying that you were propositioning me?" she demanded incredulously. To her irritation, he actually laughed at the question.

"I must admit the thought did cross my mind," he said. "You are a lovely, desirable woman. And it occurred to me that Lyndon would not be above using you as a lure to keep me around."

"So you were testing your theory?"

"Perhaps," he said noncommittally.

"Were you surprised by the answer?"

"Not really."

Kelly was surprised by his answer. She was even more surprised by his next words. "I had a feeling that no matter what Lyndon's intentions might have been, you'd never go along with them. In fact, I'm willing to bet you were even unaware of them when you took the job. Am I right?"

"Yes."

"Does he know how you feel about his little scheme?"

"I've made him aware of my opinion of his tactics," she said.

"I'll bet that was quite a conversation, Miss Patrick," Grant said, chuckling at the thought. "Lyndon probably never suspected what a temper you hide beneath that cool façade."

He studied her intently for several minutes, his eyes traveling lazily over her body, taking in the curves that were revealed all too clearly through the thin material of her caftan. Kelly's pulse raced, and a warm glow seemed to radiate from some molten core deep inside her. Her earlier wariness and outrage began to fade, replaced by some deeper and far more powerful emotion. Then he spoke.

"Spend the weekend with me," he suggested in a low voice, husky with desire.

"What?" she shouted, leaping to her feet. "I thought we'd just settled all that." Shaking with fury, she gestured toward the door. "Get out of here! Now!"

Instantly, he was on his feet in front of her. "Wait," he pleaded softly. His hands reached toward her, but stopped just inches from touching her. "I meant let's spend the weekend getting to know each other. Let's start all over. I'll show you around Chicago. We can go to the zoo, sail on Lake Michigan, whatever you'd like."

"And that's all?" she asked insistently, still suspicious.

"That's all," he promised.

There was something in his voice, in the way he was looking at her that made Kelly believe him.

"Okay," she agreed at last. Then, deciding that she held the advantage for the moment, she pressed, "But what about the contract? You said the terms were fair. Are you ready to sign it?"

"Not on your life, boss lady," he said with a bold grin as he moved toward the door. "We've just begun to negotiate. You've made your offer, but I have a few ideas of my own about the terms I want in this deal."

"Want to tell me what they are?" she asked, following him to the door and gazing up at him.

He lifted his hand to run a finger lightly along the cheek of her upturned face. "No way," he said softly. "We wouldn't want the game to end this easily, would we? Good night, boss lady."

Before Kelly realized what he intended, he leaned down and kissed her gently, his lips meeting hers in nothing more than a sweet gesture of affection. But what began so innocently swiftly became charged with a degree of electricity that brought Kelly swaying toward Grant. She might have fallen had he not caught her in his strong arms and crushed her against his chest, a soft moan escaping his lips as he brought them once more against hers.

This time there was an undeniable hunger to the kiss. Kelly's lips parted and her own tongue tasted first his lips and then, as they opened, reached inside to meet his searching tongue. This breathless exchange came upon them both with such a sudden, unexpected force that it seemed to sap them of any strength at all and their bodies clung together in mutual support and growing desire.

Kelly could feel every inch of her skin responding to the heat that radiated from Grant's body. It seemed to sear her through the caftan's barely concealing fabric. Her unconfined breasts, instantly tingling and fully aroused, strained toward him, seeking a touch that, so far, he denied her. Instead, his hands remained fixed firmly on her waist, as though he were undecided about whether to pull her more tightly to him in an irrevocable gesture of passion or to set her aside.

At last, with a reluctance she could sense and share, he stepped away from her, shaking his head, a bemused expression on his face.

"I'm sorry," he apologized. "That wasn't supposed to happen."

Kelly stood before him feeling oddly bereft without his body next to hers. "But it did," she said slowly, unable to keep a touch of wonder from her voice.

"It won't happen again, boss lady. I promise you that," he said with conviction, though the light blazing in his eyes as they met hers contradicted his words.

"Not even if I want it to?" Kelly asked quietly, still confused by the emotions that kiss had unleashed in her.

He smiled slowly at her words and his voice was gentle when he responded. "Not even if you want it to, golden girl. It's not part of the deal, remember?"

With that, he opened the door and walked out, leaving Kelly to stare after him. Feeling more vulnerable than she had ever felt before, she trembled at the memory of Grant's touch. It was awakening her in a way she'd never experienced, in a way she had always feared. Now, though, her fears seemed to center on the possibility that Grant would stick to his word and withhold that touch. That realization confused her almost as much as being in his arms had excited her. For the first time in her life the thought of going to bed alone made her feel incredibly empty.

CHAPTER FIVE

The rest of the week flew by at a dizzying pace as Kelly began a round of meetings with the station's department heads. Questioning them closely about every detail of the operation, probing for their ideas about long overdue changes needed to assure continued growth, she proved to most of them that she was not only an apt student, but a born leader. Her management style reassured and inspired them. By Friday there remained only a handful of executives who were skeptical about Lyndon Phillips's choice.

But, while Kelly was proud of winning over most of the staff so skillfully and even though she immersed herself in work, the firm, masculine features of Grant Andrews continued to dominate her thoughts. Twice a day, early evening and late at night, she stopped whatever she was doing to turn on the news. Those ritualistic glimpses, however fleeting, nurtured her memory of Monday night and the way she had responded to his kiss.

That memory was both thrilling and troublesome. The woman so long sublimated by her drive and ambition was emerging, yielding to long-unexplored feelings. Why, though, did the man responsible for the arousal of those feelings have to be Grant Andrews of all people? He was a local celebrity in a business prone to gossip and, worse than that, he was a man with whom she still must negotiate a crucial contract. Any personal relationship between them carried with it the very real threat of being labeled by many as a conflict of interest.

Despite that, Kelly found herself wondering if Grant would follow up on his promise to show her around town this weekend. It was already Friday afternoon and he hadn't called. Perhaps he, too, had thought better of the whole thing.

As she sat at her desk trying to concentrate on the fall programing schedule in front of her, the office door opened and Janie came in, her fresh-scrubbed young face alight with excitement. She was holding an arrangement of deep blue irises.

"These just came for you, Miss Patrick. Aren't they gorgeous?"

Kelly, who'd had more than her share of long-stemmed red roses from unimaginative suitors, agreed. "They are lovely. Is there a card?"

Janie handed her the small white envelope, put the flowers on a corner of the desk, and then waited hopefully while Kelly read the card.

The message was scrawled in a bold, masculine handwriting: "Here's something to match your eyes, golden girl. Until Saturday." He had signed the card "Mr. Andrews," mocking her Saturday edict that they should stick to a formal, businesslike form of address.

"Who're they from, Miss Patrick?" Janie asked when she could stand it no more.

Kelly smiled at the girl's curiosity, but she wasn't about to satisfy it and have rumors flying around the station before the end of the day. "Just a friend," she said noncommittally.

"Must be some friend," Janie muttered, not bothering to mask her disappointment over her boss's secrecy.

Moments later Kelly's private line rang. When she answered, the deep, provocative voice on the other end was unmistakable.

"Hi, boss lady. Did you get my present?"

"Yes, and they're lovely," Kelly said, warming to the sound of his voice.

"Do we still have a date for the weekend?"

"If you don't mind playing tour guide, I'd love it," she said sincerely. "I do have to spend some time tomorrow looking at apartments though."

"Good, I'll help. What time is your first appointment?"

"Nine o'clock, but you really don't need to go with me. You'll be bored to tears. Wouldn't you rather meet someplace later?"

"Nope. I have a thing about closets and views. I can't bear the thought of your not getting the best of both."

Kelly laughed at the seriousness of his tone. "I can

understand your concern about the view, but closets?"

"Closets, love, are very important," he lectured, adding with feigned sorrow, "Alas, I came to that realization somewhat belatedly. I took an apartment without checking for closets and discovered to my horror that it had only one, which held two suits, four shirts, and an umbrella if you crammed things in. After six months of hanging the rest of my clothes on the shower rod, stacking the sheets and towels in a corner of the bedroom, and keeping the vacuum cleaner under the dining room table, where I hoped visitors would think it was a piece of pop art, I swore never again to take an apartment without a full complement of walk-in closets, linen closets, and utility closets."

"I get the picture," she said. "Perhaps I do need your advice after all."

"In that case, I'll pick you up at your hotel at eight thirty."

"Fine. See you then."

"Good-bye, boss lady," he said softly, the inflection in his voice like a gentle caress.

Despite her doubts about the wisdom of getting any closer to Grant, and despite the angry sparks that occasionally flew during their conversations, it was the tenderness she heard in his tone, the brief flashes of sensitivity and humor that remained with Kelly throughout the rest of the afternoon and evening. By Saturday morning she found herself anxious to see him again.

She was up at the crack of dawn, every sense feeling alive and alert to the possibilities of the day. Dressing in a denim split skirt that revealed her shapely calves, a cotton knit top that fell loosely over the curves of her breasts, and a pair of espadrilles she hoped would allow her to keep pace with Grant's long strides, she looked fashionably casual and far more feminine than she ever did in the office.

While eating the toast and scrambled eggs she'd ordered from room service, she glanced through the *Times,* checking the television page to see if there'd been any comments by the critics about the station. She'd been studying the style of the paper's primary columnist all week, hoping to get a fix on his tactics. The promotion department had arranged for the man to interview her next week and she wanted to be prepared. This morning, however, the only column was by the back-up critic.

Kelly had tossed the paper aside and was making a list of the appointments she'd made with rental agents, when Grant arrived.

"Morning, golden girl. You all set to go exploring?" he asked when she opened the door to let him in. For a moment she couldn't respond, as her eyes raked boldly over his body. He was wearing a forest green knit shirt that molded itself to his broad chest and muscular shoulders before tapering to his slim waist. His jeans, too, were far more revealing than the looser-fitting suits she'd seen him in. He had the long-legged, trim build of the basketball player he'd once been. His obvious virility took her breath away.

Finally, shakily, she managed to say, "Sure. Come on in while I get my purse and a sweater."

"Where's your list of apartments?" he called out to her as she disappeared into the bedroom.

"On the table."

When she returned, he was looking it over and nodding his head. "You've picked the right area," he said approvingly of the prestigious addresses along Lake Shore Drive. "Are you planning to rent or buy?"

"With interest rates the way they are, I'd rather rent for a year," she told him. "But if the deal's good enough, I may go ahead and buy now, especially if I fall in love with the apartment."

"Just be sure you don't let the agent know you've fallen in love with the place," he warned. "The prices are bad enough, even when you hate it."

Moments later they were on their way in Grant's surprisingly sedate though expensive foreign economy car. Kelly had expected something flashier than the cream-colored Toyota Cressida. Apparently there was a conservative side to the anchorman, a side that ran counter to his image as a swinging bachelor-about-town.

As they sped along the lakefront, Kelly reveled in the beauty of the day. The morning air was still cool, but with the promise of warmth from the bright sun. Lake Michigan shimmered under the glow, and the horizon was dotted with splashes of color as sailboats raced along on the wind.

"I don't think I ever realized how truly beautiful Chicago is," she told Grant.

"It is something, isn't it? But don't let its summer deceive you. Come winter you'll understand why it's known as the Windy City. When the snow piles up and the temperatures drop, you'll think you've moved to Alaska. It's difficult to remember all this when you're bracing against a blizzard."

"Sort of like trying to remember the warmth of a lover's touch once the fire of passion has died?" Kelly suggested lightly as Grant looked at her in surprise.

"Exactly."

For several minutes they each seemed lost in their own memories. At last Grant spoke. "You know, boss lady, sometimes you amaze me."

Kelly looked at him and smiled tentatively. "Lately I seem to be amazing myself," she said softly, the words hanging in the air between them like some sort of unfulfilled promise.

Then the moment was lost as they arrived at the first of Kelly's addresses. It was a towering skyscraper that held the promise of spectacular views. The real estate agent was waiting for them in the lobby.

"Miss Patrick, it's so nice to meet you," the striking brunette said, barely shaking Kelly's hand before turning her attention to Grant. "Mr. Andrews, I'd recognize you anywhere," she gushed, her business-like demeanor replaced by a low, feminine purr. "I think you're marvelous."

"Thanks. It's nice of you to say so," he responded

warmly. Kelly noticed, though, that the smile on his lips didn't quite reach his eyes. His reaction to the woman was courteous and nothing more. Obviously, he was used to this sort of adulation and found it, if not distasteful, somewhat uncomfortable.

Grant's presence did provide one unexpected benefit Kelly discovered once they were in the apartment. The agent was so preoccupied with the anchorman that Kelly was left on her own to explore the apartment and form her own impression without having to suffer through a sales pitch. The rooms were large and sunny, the kitchen spacious and very modern. There was even a view of the lake. She tried to picture the place with her furniture, with plants basking in the filtered sunlight, with her small collection of paintings on the walls. In her mind's eye it all seemed to fit.

Recalling what Grant had told her, though, she remained noncommittal in discussing terms with the agent. She noted dimensions in a small notebook, the possibility of a lease-option arrangement, straight rental terms, and the owner's asking price should she decide to buy.

"Thanks for your time," she told the woman a half-hour later. "I'll be in touch."

"It was a pleasure," the agent assured Kelly, her eyes never leaving Grant. Her meaning was so obvious it was all Kelly could do to keep from laughing. Instead, though, she managed to say dryly, "Yes, I'm sure it was."

Back in the car she and Grant looked at each other

and burst out laughing. "Is it always like that?" she asked.

"No," he said. "Sometimes it's worse."

"How on earth could it be any worse? That woman was ready to throw you on the floor and attack you right in front of me."

Grant grinned at her. "Yes. But at least she didn't try it."

"You mean some do?" Kelly was incredulous.

He nodded. "I'm afraid so."

"Does it bother you?" she asked curiously, then added daringly, "or do you love every minute of it?"

"I hate it. But it comes with the job. Without those women, your newscast wouldn't be on top in the ratings. You'll learn to appreciate it too."

"I doubt it," Kelly said, shaking her head. "How do you ever have any privacy?"

"Stick with me, boss lady, and I'll show you," he said tauntingly. "You can always escape if you want to badly enough."

Fortunately, the next real estate agent was a man and, although he was clearly impressed by Grant, he was thoroughly professional, concentrating all of his energy on demonstrating his vast knowledge of Chicago property values and explaining why his particular apartment was the very best on the market. To Grant's amusement and Kelly's absolute fury, however, he made his pitch to the anchorman. Though he knew Kelly was the potential buyer, he was obviously convinced that a woman would never understand such things as variable mortgage rates, monthly maintenance charges, and the building's energy-saving features.

Kelly found the apartment oppressive and overpriced. Angry at the agent's treatment, though, she interrupted the flow of his monologue.

"I'd like to see some figures on the exact escalation of property values in this neighborhood over the last five years, the taxes being paid on these apartments, a maintenance record on the common areas of the building and, if it's not too much trouble, the exact monthly payments, including taxes and maintenance charges with twenty percent down and a twenty-nine-year mortgage."

The man stared at her, then back at Grant. The anchorman shrugged. "As we told you, she's the buyer," he said.

"Correction," Kelly said. "She might have been the buyer. You, sir, lost her with your chauvinistic assumption that it was the man you needed to impress. You might want to keep that in mind the next time you discuss terms with a prospective client."

With that, she turned and flounced from the apartment, adding a deliberately provocative sway to her hips. Grant followed her, leaving the agent to stare helplessly after them.

Kelly was waiting for him on the sidewalk in front of the building, tapping her foot impatiently. "Of all the arrogant, stupid . . ." she began, her temper exploding.

"Miss Patrick," Grant said soothingly, his eyes bright with laughter, "I'd say you made your point."

As her eyes met his twinkling ones, her blazing fury died. "Sorry," she said. "That attitude just makes me so damn mad."

"So I gathered. Now shall we try again, or do you want to call it a day?"

"No. I'm not giving up yet. There are two more apartments on my list."

"Okay, then. Let's get on with it."

Neither of the remaining apartments measured up to the first one they had seen and, despite her reaction to the agent's blatant overtures to Grant, Kelly was growing more and more inclined to take it.

"Why do you have to decide on one of them today?" Grant argued, when she told him her decision.

"I can't stay in that hotel suite forever."

"No, but you don't need to be out tomorrow either. Take another week and look around some more. There are more and more condominiums coming on the market, and right now is a good time to buy because the sellers are usually anxious to get out."

Puzzled by the intensity in his voice, Kelly asked, "Didn't you like that first apartment?"

"It was fine. I just think you can do better."

"Are you sure that's all? It had a view . . . and lots of closets."

"Okay. Okay," he said wearily. "Take it if you want to."

Kelly fell silent. What was going on here, she wondered. Why was Grant suddenly in such a temper over her choice of an apartment? It didn't make any sense.

"So," he said finally, "Do you want to call the agent and tell her you'll take it?"

"No," she said slowly. "Maybe you're right. I'll think about it for a few more days." Perhaps, she thought to herself, in that time she could figure out Grant's strange reaction.

Whatever had caused it, though, seemed to disappear the moment she agreed to wait before calling the agent. His mood lightened as he suggested they go to lunch and then for a walk in Lincoln Park.

"Sounds perfect," she agreed. "I'm famished."

He took her to a small restaurant specializing in crepes. Though the place was crowded and people recognized Grant immediately, they left them alone. They ordered a carafe of Chablis to go with their seafood crepes and for dessert they shared a sinfully caloric crepe filled with ice cream and topped with a maple pecan sauce and whipped cream.

"I don't think I can move," Kelly said with a satisfied sigh.

"In that case, I'm very sorry we're in a public place," Grant teased. "It might be nice to try to seduce a lady who can't slip away from me."

"I thought you'd decided I was off limits," she said softly.

"You are," he said, a finger gently tracing a line down her arm, leaving a path of fire in its wake. "But life is full of contradictions and this seems to be one of them."

"Meaning?"

"Meaning that you are still strictly off limits," he told her, his eyes caressing her where his hands dared not. "But I definitely don't have to like it."

"If I don't like it either, couldn't we change the rules?" Kelly asked softly, her body betraying her with its yearning for a more intimate exploration, even as her head told her that Grant was right.

"I'm afraid not, love," he said regretfully. "There's too much at stake."

Though his words were firm, the smoldering passion in his eyes told another story, a story that held a promise for the future. Kelly trembled at the depth of her need for that promise to be fulfilled.

CHAPTER SIX

Kelly sat, her back against the gnarled trunk of a huge shade tree, relishing the cool breeze that played over her flushed cheeks. Grant lay stretched out face-down on the grass beside her. His long silence and the steady, even pattern of his breathing suggested he had fallen asleep in the aftermath of their lunch and their walk through the park.

They had covered a lot of ground in the last couple of hours, she thought, sighing contentedly and allowing her own eyes to drift shut against the bright glare of the sun reflecting from the lake. It wasn't just that they had walked for miles. They had really talked for the first time since they had met. All the barriers, the pretenses, and the cautions had seemed to disappear as they shared their experiences and their interests.

They had discovered a common love of good jazz, though Grant preferred the wild beat of drums, while Kelly tended toward the more lyrical musical adventures of the flute. She had a feeling that that was symptomatic of the differences in their personalities.

Grant was all predatory male, while, despite her ambitions, she had the heart of a romantic.

Their tastes were more similar in films and plays. Both of them liked the escape of light comedies. Given a choice between a flawed Neil Simon romp on stage or screen and an Oscar-winning foreign film, heavy with significance, they'd opt for the comedy every time. Their lives, they agreed, were already filled with far too much reality.

What had surprised Kelly the most about Grant's widely varied interests, however, was his professed love of reading. While she envisioned him blazing a trail through the hottest Chicago nightspots, he painted another picture entirely, that of a man who liked nothing better than to spend an evening with a stack of magazines or a complicated thriller. Someday, he'd told her, he wanted to go off to a cottage by the ocean for a few months and write a book himself. He was convinced he could weave a plot of international intrigue as well as John le Carré or Robert Ludlum.

"Every journalist thinks he can turn his writing skill into a best seller," he'd told her with a grin. "Most of them, though, have the good sense not to try."

"What do you mean? Shouldn't everyone try to fulfill their secret ambitions?"

"Not always. Some ambitions are doomed to failure."

"Is failure so bad?" Kelly had wondered.

"It is when it spoils a perfectly good dream."

Kelly thought about those words as she glanced over at the still form next to her. Had there been a subtle warning implied in the lightly spoken phrase? Would the reality of a relationship between them ruin what was beginning to seem such a bright and promising dream? She had already had doubts about the wisdom of becoming emotionally entangled with Grant. Clearly, he shared those doubts. Twice now he had withdrawn from her just as their bodies had been leading them toward a greater intimacy. She knew he wanted her as much as she was beginning to yearn for him, yet he refused to yield to those feelings. Perhaps he had already concluded there could be no long-term future for them and that without it a transitory fling would be painful and self-defeating.

Grant moaned softly and rolled onto his side. She studied the man who seemed to have taken such a firm grip on her thoughts in such a short time. It had been only a week since Lyndon Phillips's party and yet it felt as though Grant had been part of her life forever. No one had ever staked a claim on her so completely. No one had ever aroused her senses so thoroughly by the merest touch. Other lovers, using far more practiced skill, had never spurred her responsiveness to the heights to which she suspected Grant could take her.

She reached over to brush a blade of grass from his cheek. Her fingers lingered, reveling in the warmth of his flesh, in the roughness of the evening shadow of a beard that was beginning to appear. Unable to draw away, she traced the outline of his lips, gasping when he suddenly seized her hand and kissed the open palm. His mouth was like a searing brand against her skin.

"How long have you been taking advantage of me, while I slept?" he mumbled hoarsely, still holding tightly to her hand.

"Is that what I was doing?" she asked innocently.

"You know perfectly well it was," he said, his eyes roving slowly over her, drinking in the rise and fall of her breasts. "That's a dangerous game, Miss Patrick."

"Only if you can't afford the stakes," she said.

"Sweetheart, neither one of us can afford the stakes in this one," he retorted, the look in his eyes softening the effect of his words.

"You afraid I'll talk you out of a few thousand dollars or your on-air wardrobe?" she taunted lightly. Her desire to break through his determination to keep a wall between them made her daring. "I promise to keep our negotiations separate from our private life. We should be adult enough to do that."

He looked at her skeptically. "It's these very adult feelings I have for you at this moment that convince me I'm right. Good negotiations require artful diplomacy, not total capitulation, Miss Patrick."

There was something in his tone, a hint of bitterness perhaps, that made Kelly withdraw her hand from his grasp. "Are we back to that again?" she asked.

"Back to what?"

"Back to the fact that you don't trust my motives in wanting to be close to you."

Grant sighed heavily and sat up. He reached out and lightly stroked her cheek in a tender gesture that made her heart begin to race. Unwilling to face him and reveal how easily he affected her senses, she kept her eyes cast down until he forced her to meet his gaze.

"Kelly, this is an impossible situation and you know it," he said slowly and firmly, though she thought she detected a flash of pain in his eyes. "You're my boss. You want something from me. How can I ever be sure whether you're acting in your own interests or in the interest of Phillips Broadcasting?"

Stung by the realization that he could actually have such doubts about her, Kelly lashed back, "And how am I supposed to know whether you care about me or about how much you can get in your new contract? The suspicions work both ways, you know."

"That's exactly my point. Neither of us can ever be entirely sure. What sort of relationship could we possibly build with those doubts always there between us?"

Convinced by the logic of his words, Kelly suddenly laughed, though there was a harsh edge to the sound. Grant gave her a questioning look.

"I was just thinking about what you said at the party the other night," she told him. "You said Lyndon was down in Dallas pulling all the strings. Well, he certainly seems to have the two of us dancing to his tune, doesn't he?"

As she spoke, Kelly was assailed by a powerful sense of loss. It was as though someone had held a magnificent jewel in front of her, taunting her with its brilliance, then snatched it away again, denying her the right to share in its beauty. She knew it was useless to argue with Grant about this. Her pride would not even allow her to try. Besides, he was right. Somehow she must learn to accept the limitations that circumstances had imposed on their relationship. She must learn to think of him as an employee, possibly even as a valued friend, but nothing more.

The sun was beginning to sink in the cloudless afternoon sky and the shadows were lengthening. The breeze from the lake had a bite to it, chilling her body just as the last few moments seemed to have frozen her heart. Unable to bear another moment with the thoughts of what might have been, she said, "I think we'd better call it a day. I've got some work to go over tonight."

Grant nodded. He got to his feet and pulled her up. For a moment they were only inches apart, their eyes locked in the embrace that they'd forbidden to their bodies. Kelly was the first to look away. She didn't want Grant to see the desire that tormented her. When he took her hand as they strolled slowly back to his car, she didn't resist. It was as though she were powerless to deny herself at least this much when she yearned for so much more.

The drive back along Michigan Avenue seemed endless, though it took only a few minutes. Neither of them spoke, apparently sensing that there was nothing else to be said for the moment. However, when Grant pulled up in front of the hotel, he got out of the car and came around to open her door.

Awkwardly, Kelly held out her hand. "Thanks for a lovely day, Grant. I really do appreciate your going with me to look at apartments and showing me around the city."

Grant's expression hardened at the cool politeness of her words. He handed the car keys to the doorman and grasped her elbow firmly, guiding her into the building.

"Grant, I can see myself upstairs," she protested.

"I'm perfectly aware of your self-sufficiency," he replied, his voice mocking.

"Then, why . . . ?"

"I wish to God I knew," he muttered harshly, following her into the elevator. The scowl on his face effectively silenced Kelly, even if she could have thought of a response to the strange mix of anger and despair she thought she heard in his voice.

Inside the suite, he mixed himself a drink, then began pacing around the room. He seemed to have forgotten her existence as he stalked through the limited space, pausing occasionally to stare moodily out the window. Kelly sat on the sofa watching him, puzzled by the tension evident in his odd behavior. For a man who normally appeared to be in total control of himself, this uncertainty, this barely contained anger was totally uncharacteristic.

"Come here," he said at last, so softly that at first Kelly wasn't certain he had spoken at all. When he repeated the request, there was a hard urgency in his voice.

Kelly stood and went to him, her pulse racing with an expectancy she couldn't explain. When he turned to her, there was such a burning intensity in his eyes that her heart began to pound. He reached out and brushed a stray curl from her forehead and Kelly noticed with a sense of amazement that his hand was shaking. She wanted desperately to take his hand in her own and hold it tightly, but she knew she didn't dare. Grant seemed to be fighting some sort of inner battle, and instinct told her she had to let him decide its outcome.

Finally, when she thought she couldn't bear another instant of suspense, he groaned and pulled her into his arms. Pressed tightly against him, her breasts crushed against his chest, her hips held firmly to his, Kelly could feel the throbbing passion that coursed through his body in trembling waves. By the time he brought his lips down on hers, every inch of her body was already under his command. Her mouth yielded readily to his intimate assault, her tongue as anxious as his to explore this sweet new territory. His mouth was a curious mix of fiery heat and cold. His lips burned against hers, but inside she could feel the cool trail of ice left by his drink and taste the faint trace of Scotch. The effect was as intoxicating as any champagne.

Grant's hands massaged the taut muscles of her shoulders, then slid slowly down her back, coming to rest on her hips. Kelly's flesh was on fire everywhere he touched it, despite the fabric that kept the heat of his probing, exploring fingers from her skin.

"Take my shirt off," he whispered, his voice a husky command. Tentatively she pulled the fabric free from the waistband of his jeans and, with his help, lifted it over his head and tossed it aside. Her fingers began an exploration of their own, trailing across the hair-rough expanse of his chest, lingering in the center where she could feel the pounding of his heart, which seemed to match the erratic cadence of her own. He moaned softly as she lowered her head and lightly touched each firm nipple with her tongue.

Her arms around his waist, their bodies pressed tightly together, she lifted her eyes to meet his, recognizing the hunger and longing she saw there. The doubts, for the moment anyway, seemed to have disappeared, hidden by the overpowering shadow of passion.

"This is right, Grant," she murmured breathlessly. "It has to be."

"I hope you're right," he said, as though all sense of logic had been dazed by a desire he could no longer control.

"Please," she urged. "No more talking. No more doubts."

He scooped her into his arms then and carried her

into the bedroom. When she would have removed her skirt and top, he pushed aside her hands and slowly undressed her himself. For Kelly it was a slow, tormenting ritual as he lingered over the task that she would have rushed to complete.

He placed her gently on the bed, then stood gazing down at her, as though admiring an exquisite work of art. It was as though he wanted to absorb every detail about her, from the tousled curls to the pale shoulders, from the full breasts with their aroused pink centers to the flat stomach, from the softly rounded thighs to the long, tapering calves. As his intense gaze touched each exposed part of her, Kelly felt a mounting excitement that seemed to center in her abdomen and radiate throughout her body. By the time he lowered himself beside her, she was ready for him as she had never been ready for any other man.

Her skin protested against the jeans, which kept them from a total fulfillment, and her hands trembled as she tried to remove them from him. Grant seemed intent on prolonging the expectancy, however. He determinedly refused to assist her, continuing instead to tease and arouse her body until she ached for a release she knew could only come with the ultimate union with his body.

Apparently sensing her frustration, Grant allowed her awakened senses to slowly drift back from the peak of excitement to which he'd carried them. Slipping off his jeans and briefs, he urged her to begin her own brand of seduction, encouraging the demanding forays of her anxious hands, the sweet, tender caresses of her moist lips. Slowly he began matching her escalating pace, responding as her body arched toward his, seeking satisfaction. No longer could either of them deny the feverish pitch of their arousal and with a shuddering moan they came together, their bodies blending in near-perfect harmony. It was for each of them the wild beating of drums and soaring beauty of the flute playing in concert.

It had been exactly the way Kelly had known it would be. She and Grant were in tune, the chemistry between them a sensuous mix of physical attraction and intellectual compatibility. Even now, as a pleasant languor was stealing over them, their bodies were attuned. It would take the merest spark to ignite the flame of passion between them all over again.

Kelly ran her hand lightly over the hard muscle of Grant's thigh, where it rested across her own. She could feel it tense beneath her touch and hear the sudden quickening of his breathing.

"You aren't by any chance one of those insatiable seductresses I've heard about?" he asked softly.

"I'm not sure," she teased. "I was just wondering about finding out."

"So I'm your guinea pig."

"I wouldn't have put it quite that way," she said, pausing to nibble on his ear. "But you certainly do seem to be a willing subject."

He rolled over on top of her, pinning her to the bed. "Oh, I'm more than willing," he murmured against her lips before claiming them in a crushing kiss that left them both breathless. "I don't know what you're doing to me, Kelly Patrick," he said as his fingers circled her breasts, stroking and teasing until the nipples hardened into sensitive peaks. Kelly gasped as a wave of pleasure washed over her just from the intensity of that touch.

"I don't know who's doing what to whom," she said, her voice a ragged whisper. "It seems to have gotten all mixed up."

Once more their bodies were tangled together, their hands, lips, and teeth creating an intimate pattern of merciless arousal until once again they came together in a soaring, shuddering explosion of pleasure. When it was over, they slept, cradled in each other's arms.

Darkness had fallen and the only light in the room came from the glow of the digital clock by the bedside. It was 9:32, Kelly noted, when the shrill ringing of the phone jarred her awake. She stretched across Grant to try to grab the receiver, but he stopped her.

"Let it ring," he muttered sleepily. "They'll take a message at the desk."

Kelly was tempted to give in, but the phone's insistent ringing showed no sign of abating. "I'd better get it, Grant. It might be important," she said, trying to ignore the way he was nuzzling her neck.

"Hello," she said, trying to muffle a gasp as Grant nipped her earlobe.

"Kelly, darlin', how are you?" boomed the unmistakable voice of Lyndon Phillips. Kelly grimaced. He was the last person she wanted to talk to right now.

"I'm just fine, Mr. Phillips," she said as sweetly as she could manage. "What can I do for you?"

"I just thought I'd call and see how our little project is movin' along. You got that anchorman eating out of your hand yet?"

Grant had frozen beside her and Kelly could tell he had heard every incriminating word.

"Mr. Andrews and I have been meeting," she replied stiffly, watching in dismay as Grant slipped from the bed and began pulling on his clothes. "I told you I'd keep you informed about the progress of the negotiations. I promise I'll call you as soon as I have something definite to report."

"Kelly, don't you waste any time on this," Mr. Phillips warned her again. "Grant Andrews is nobody's fool. You'll have to take command of the situation from the very beginning."

Kelly knew she had lost more than her command of the contract negotiations as Grant stalked from the bedroom. Desperate to salvage something from a day that had seesawed between doubts and hope and, finally, risen above them both to an unexpectedly thrilling fulfillment, she cut Lyndon Phillips off in mid-sentence.

"I'm sorry, sir, but this isn't a very good time for me. I'll have to speak with you later." With his protests still ringing in her ear, she slammed down the receiver and rushed from the room. Grant was just finishing tucking his shirt into his jeans.

"Grant, please," she implored, the dim light shining from the bedroom behind her making her body glow like alabaster. A brief flash of warmth flickered in his eyes as they roved over her, but it was gone in an instant, replaced with something cold and hard. He had obviously made his judgment about her and there would be no trial, no appeal.

"See you around, boss lady," he said, sarcasm making his voice a harsh whip that seemed to sting her flesh. "I must say the negotiations have been . . . interesting. Next time maybe I should bring along my agent. Perhaps he'd like to see how you operate."

"How *I* operate? You're the one who insisted on coming up here."

"You didn't seem opposed to the possibility when we were in the park. One more tactical maneuver, Ms. Patrick? Make the poor sucker think it was all his own idea?"

Kelly flinched at the bitterness in his tone. "You know damn well that whatever happened today between us had nothing to do with your contract," she charged angrily.

"How do I know that?"

"Because—because that's not the way I do business," she insisted, helpless to think of a way to convince him, to wipe the look of near-hatred from his eyes.

"You'll understand if I have difficulty buying that, I'm sure," he said coldly, opening the door. "You can return that call to Lyndon now. Tell him the negotiations have broken down. I'm sure he'll have some ideas about what you should do next."

He walked out then, closing the door very softly behind him. The sound cut through Kelly just as though he had slammed it. There was something very final about it.

CHAPTER SEVEN

Tom Winston, the station's aggressive young promotion manager, was in Kelly's office going over the final preparations for the fall season campaign. He spread mechanicals for the newspaper ads out on her desk and explained how each one took the network theme and carried it through to include their own local programs.

"That theme is picked up in the on-air spots as well. I think it's the best campaign we've put together in years," he told her enthusiastically. "Would you like to take a look at the thirty-second promo now?"

There was a silence for several seconds before Kelly looked at him distractedly and apologized. "Tom, I'm sorry. What did you say? My mind seems to be on something else."

"That's okay, Miss Patrick. I just asked if you wanted to take a look at any of the on-air spots."

"Sure," she said, forcing her attention back to the business at hand as Tom put the tape into her video cassette player and turned it on. The promotional spots were upbeat and slickly produced, she thought as the images flashed across the screen. The fleeting glimpses of the series' stars were interwoven with location shots in Chicago of the station's own celebrities, including Grant in front of City Hall, where he was conducting an interview with the mayor. Kelly felt a stabbing pain in the region of her heart at the sight of him, but she covered her inner turmoil by telling Tom how terrific she thought the spots were.

"You've done a great job. How soon are we going to start airing them?"

"I thought we'd go with the generic ones covering all of the shows beginning next week. Then we can start hitting on the specific series in late August to build up to the premieres in September."

"Good. I looked over your budget figures the other day. Are you sure you've allowed enough for a strong newspaper and magazine campaign in September?"

Tom looked at her in amazement. "I've never had anyone suggest I might be spending too little money before."

Kelly laughed. "It's not that I want you to spend more. I'd just rather know now if you think you're going to go over-budget."

"No. I think the figures are realistic."

"Fine. Just remember I'd always prefer that to a soft estimate you can't possibly hope to stick with."

"You've got it, Miss Patrick," he promised as the intercom buzzed.

"What is it, Janie?"

"I know you said you didn't want to be disturbed, but Mr. Phillips is here and he insists on seeing you right now," she said breathlessly just as Kelly's door burst open and the tall Texan strode into the room.

"It's okay, Janie," Kelly soothed the panic-stricken girl. "After all, Mr. Phillips does own this place. I suppose he has a right to make his presence felt, no matter what he might be interrupting."

Though her voice was filled with sarcasm, she could tell it was lost on her boss as he lowered himself into one of the comfortable, thickly cushioned armchairs across from her and puffed on his cigar, sending swirls of foul-smelling smoke into the air. Kelly ignored him and turned back to Tom, who was gathering up his promotional layouts and tapes.

"When you have a final schedule for all of this, get it to me," she requested. "We may want to do a little more in the suburban papers."

"Okay, Miss Patrick. I'll have it on your desk by tomorrow," he said, nodding in Lyndon Phillips's direction as he left.

Slowly, trying to contain her irritation, Kelly faced the older man, whose face by now was flushed with anger. "What can I do for you?" she asked calmly. "I assume it's something important since you chose to barge in here in the middle of a meeting."

"Don't you go gettin' uppity with me, my dear," he warned. "Like you told that gal out there, I do own this place."

"And you've hired me to run it for you," Kelly countered.

"For the moment," he reminded her harshly as their eyes locked in a test of wills. After several interminable minutes he laughed loudly, the hoarse boom filling the room. "You do have spunk, Kelly Patrick. I knew you were a spitfire when I hired you. Just didn't expect you to be firing it at me."

"Why should I make you an exception?" she inquired sweetly. "It's not in my character to let anyone push me around, any more than it's in yours."

"Guess that's why I took to you," he said in a calmer tone. "We are a lot alike. Now, tell me what's been happening with Grant Andrews. I didn't like the sound of things when we talked the other day."

"So you flew up here to check it out personally? Your faith in me is touching."

"It's got nothing to do with any lack of faith in you. I just thought I'd come on up here and take you out to dinner and see if there's anything I can do to help you iron out any problems you might be havin' with the negotiations. I do have some experience in this sort of thing," he added dryly.

"I see," Kelly said, marveling anew at his ability to flatter her for her business acumen one minute, then retract it through his actions the next.

"Besides," he told her, ignoring the sarcasm in her tone, "there's a fellow up here I'd like you to meet. I've invited him to join us for dinner. He should be here any minute."

Instantly Kelly was on-guard. She had the distinct feeling Lyndon was purposely trying to catch her off-guard. She studied him warily, trying to decide what he was up to.

"Who is this man?" she asked.

"Name's David Stanton. He's a lawyer. Very bright. He'll help you learn the ropes around town, introduce you to the right people." The words were innocuous enough, but Kelly sensed there was far more going on here that the Texan wasn't saying.

"Is he on our payroll?"

"No. No, he's not connected with Phillips Broadcasting."

"Then I don't understand. Is he with the Welcome Wagon, perhaps?"

"Stop being so suspicious, woman. Can't you just relax and enjoy a night on the town?" Lyndon barked impatiently.

Kelly wanted to probe more deeply to pin Lyndon down and get a straight answer out of him, but Lyndon's attitude and the arrival of David Stanton prevented it. Janie brought the attorney into the office and Lyndon performed the introductions with a sort of forced fatherly joviality.

"It's a pleasure to meet you, Miss Patrick." David Stanton's carefully modulated voice was smoothly polite but notably devoid of warmth or sincerity. Instinctively, Kelly didn't trust the man, though he was attractive enough with his light brown hair, tan complexion, winning smile, and expensively dressed, well-toned body.

Over dinner in a Japanese restaurant, where Lyndon looked ridiculously awkward trying to accommodate his large frame to the seating on the tatami mat around the low table, the young attorney set out to charm Kelly. He was attentive and amusing, offering biting insights into the personalities of key executives at other stations in town.

In spite of her suspicions about the ulterior motive of the evening, Kelly found that she was enjoying herself. She filed away in the back of her mind the insights David was sharing with her, sensing that his astute observations would be helpful as she planned her strategy for improving the station. When the attorney offered to drive her back to her hotel, she accepted, ignoring the complacent expression she saw in Lyndon's eyes.

It wasn't until the next morning that she realized she had fallen into yet another of the Texan's traps. This one, like all the others, had been set to snare Grant Andrews, if the column on the television page of the *Times* was even partially accurate.

Blast Lyndon Phillips and his schemes, Kelly thought furiously as she scanned the devastating mix of fact and speculation about her dinner meeting with David Stanton and Lyndon. The young lawyer, it seemed, was also an agent for the midday anchorman on a competing station. Although that man's name had never even surfaced during the evening, the columnist had twisted the occasion into a bargaining session. He suggested that Lyndon Phillips and his new station manager might be looking around for a replacement for Grant Andrews, just in case the current contract talks broke down, of course.

Slamming the paper down on the table beside her untouched scrambled eggs, Kelly wasn't sure whether she was more outraged by the *Times* article's false representation of the facts or by Lyndon's deception. The whole thing was obviously a calculated effort on his part to give them additional leverage with Grant. He'd probably even tipped off the columnist himself.

Couldn't he see what sort of havoc this would create? If Grant hadn't trusted her before, this would only further confirm his belief that she was nothing more than a conniving schemer whose only goal was to get him to sign with Phillips Broadcasting for another three years. After this he wouldn't want to deal with her at all.

Even more disturbing from Kelly's point of view was what this would do to their personal relationship. It was another rip in the fragile fabric that held them together. It could shred their relationship beyond repair.

Within ten minutes of her arrival at the office, Kelly knew that the storm she had anticipated was more likely to be a full-scale hurricane. Already there had been a flood of calls—from the media, from John Marshall, from Grant's agent, even from Lyndon. The one message she'd hoped for, however, was missing. There had been no call from Grant.

Still too angry to risk a conversation with Lyndon and unsure of what she should tell Grant's agent, she called John Marshall and asked him to come to her office. She paced the room until he arrived five minutes later, a harried expression on his face.

"Close the door," she requested as he came in, then buzzed to instruct Janie to hold all calls. "If any more reporters call, tell them I'll have a statement within the hour and we'll get back to them with it."

When she had hung up the phone, John asked quietly, "What were you thinking of, Kelly? Do you have any idea what a story like this will do to morale around here?"

"To say nothing of what it will do to our talks with Grant," she added bitterly.

Her response seemed to puzzle John. "If you realize that, why on earth did you do it?"

"Because Lyndon arranged it—the dinner, David Stanton, hell, for all I know he called the reporter himself after dessert to give a blow-by-blow rundown of the evening. Until I read the paper this morning, I had no idea who David Stanton was. His client's name was never mentioned. I didn't even know the man was an agent, much less whose. Lyndon had apparently briefed him well. If I had had any inkling of what the two of them were up to, I'd never have gone along with it."

"I'm glad to hear that," John said. "I didn't know what to think when I saw the paper this morning."

"The issue now is what we should do about it. Grant's agent has called already and I'm sure he's not going to be pacified by a few polite reassurances that it's all been a big mistake. And what about the media? What do I tell your compatriots when they call back? I've promised them a statement."

The newsman managed a weak grin. "Do you think you could tell them you think David Stanton is such an incredibly charming and sexy man that you're planning to marry him?" he suggested hopefully. "Then they just might believe that the subject of his client never came up."

Kelly gave him a withering look. "I assume you're joking. My initial reaction to David Stanton was to distrust him. Now that I know all the facts, I think he's slightly lower than a snake and only slightly less despicable than Lyndon."

"Speaking of our boss, how do you plan to handle him?" John inquired curiously.

"I'm going to suggest, as calmly as I can manage, that he go back and play in his oil fields and leave me alone to get us out of the mess he's created."

"Think he'll listen?"

"I doubt it, but it's worth a try," she said with a sigh. "Now, help me draft that statement."

Together they wrote a succinct comment, stating that the station was continuing with its negotiations with Grant Andrews in good faith and that the management was certain the anchorman would be with them for many years to come. "We are not now, nor do we expect to be, looking for a replacement. Any information to the contrary is not only speculative, but inaccurate," the statement concluded.

"Do you think they'll buy it?" Kelly asked.

"Not for a minute, but they'll have to live with it.

Once these rumors start, the only way to end them is by waving a signed contract with Grant in front of them."

"Then I'll just have to get that contract," Kelly said, trying to inject a note of optimism into her voice as she picked up the phone in response to Janie's buzz.

"Miss Patrick," she said, her voice barely above a whisper. "It's Mr. Andrews. He's out here and he seems, well, he seems a little angry. Do you want me to send him in?"

"Of course, Janie," she said, turning to John and explaining, "Grant's here."

"Do you want me to stay?"

Before Kelly could reply, Grant's cool voice sliced through the air. "No. We'd both like it if you'd leave us alone, John."

"But . . ." Kelly began, her voice trailing off at the fury she saw blazing in Grant's eyes. "Okay, have it your way. John, thanks for your help. Give that statement to Janie on your way out and tell her to have the promotion department distribute it."

"Is that about me?" Grant asked. When Kelly nodded, he said, "Mind if I take a look first?" He took the paper from her outstretched hand. A sardonic smile flitted across his features as he read it. "According to this, then, I still have a job. That's nice to know, after what I read in the paper this morning."

"Of course you still have a job here," John said quickly. "Damn it, Grant! This whole thing has been an incredible misunderstanding. I'm sure you'll see that as soon as you give Kelly a chance to explain."

"Oh, I'm sure she has the perfect explanation all planned out," he retorted sarcastically. "Lyndon probably scripted it for her."

"Grant . . ." John began.

"Never mind. Just leave us, so I can hear what she has to say."

"Sure," the news director agreed, shaking his head as he looked from one to the other of them and saw the sparks flashing in their eyes. Reluctantly, he left the office and closed the door behind him.

Kelly and Grant stood face to face, eyeing each other warily. She was determined not to be the first to look away. No matter how bad all of this looked, she knew she had done nothing wrong. Surely, she could convince him of that. He knew Lyndon Phillips as well as she did. Better, in fact. He knew what sort of ruthless tactics he was capable of trying in order to get his way. He'd believe her when she explained that this had been another one of Lyndon's schemes. At least she hoped he would, she thought, fingers crossed behind her back in a childish gesture. She'd need luck and a whole lot more to persuade him that she hadn't been in on this latest plan, that she had been as much of a victim as he.

"So," he said, breaking the long tension-filled silence at last. "What's your version?"

"The reporter put two and two together and came up with the wrong answer," she said firmly.

He regarded her skeptically. "He seems to think he's added things up and hit the jackpot."

"I repeat: He's wrong."

"Why should I believe you?"

Kelly wanted to scream, *Because I'm falling in love with you! And I would never do anything like this to you.* Instead, she said, "Because I don't resort to schemes like this to get what I want. This is Lyndon's way of doing business, not mine, and you know it."

"Oh, I recognize Lyndon's fine touch in here all right. But perhaps you're just as ambitious and ruthless as he is," he charged.

"Ambitious, yes," Kelly admitted. "I worked to get this job and I'd like to keep it, but not at the expense of using someone I . . . someone else," she retorted heatedly.

Slowly, Grant pulled a clipping of the *Times* article from his pocket and scanned it, pausing to read some of its most damning phrases aloud. When he'd finished, he looked at Kelly coldly. "I'd say the evidence against you is pretty solid, wouldn't you?"

"You'd make a terrific prosecutor. To hell with the facts. Just get the defendant," she accused. "For the record, I'd say that the evidence is all circumstantial and would fall apart under cross-examination. Care to try it, Mr. Andrews?" she challenged.

He shrugged. "Sure. Why not?"

"Want to swear me in?" she suggested sarcastically.

"I don't think that will be necessary, Miss Patrick," he said, approaching until only a slim gap remained between them. Kelly could feel the overpowering attraction of the man stealing over her traitorous body even as she stared back at him angrily. His green eyes sparkled with a dangerous gleam as he added softly, "Somehow I don't think even you are capable of looking me straight in the face and lying."

Kelly's hand moved almost involuntarily, ready to strike out in response to the derisiveness she heard in his voice. He stopped her hand only inches from his cheek. "I wouldn't do that if I were you. It will hardly help your case," he mocked.

She jerked her hand away and backed up, furious with herself for losing control. It was essential that she remain calm and businesslike. This was a professional crisis and she had to treat it as such rather than react as though she were under a personal attack. Taking a deep breath, she faced him and said quietly, "Okay. Let's get on with this. If you have questions, ask them."

As coolly and skillfully as any attorney, Grant led her through the events of the previous afternoon and evening. A part of Kelly continued to rebel at having to suffer through this absurd test of her honesty, but she could think of no other way to wipe the remaining traces of suspicion from Grant's mind. She wanted him to trust her because he cared about her and knew she was incapable of such duplicity, but deep down she knew there hadn't been sufficient time to build such trust, a trust that could withstand the sort of damning evidence that kept accumulating against her.

She responded as candidly as she could to each of Grant's questions, willing him to believe her. She thought she was beginning to detect a softening in his attitude, a warming of his voice, when the door opened and Lyndon Phillips strode in.

"Grant, my boy, Janie told me I'd find you in here," he said with hearty enthusiasm. "You here to get this contract business all settled? That piece in the paper this morning has folks around here mighty upset. Why, I had no idea what a ruckus would be caused by something like this leaking out."

Kelly sank down in the chair beside her desk and watched as Lyndon blundered on, apparently oblivious to the effect his words were having on his prize anchorman. As the pressure began to mount, Grant grew increasingly furious; his body tensed and his hands clenched. Kelly could understand his reaction. She almost shared his apparent desire to reach out and strangle their boss.

"Mr. Phillips," Grant began slowly and distinctly, making each word an indictment, "I wouldn't sign your damn contract now, if you gave me this station on a silver platter. I refuse to work for men . . . or women," he added, giving Kelly a cutting glance, "who will use any low, cheap, manipulative method to get what they want. You'd better get back to David Stanton and tell him you're interested in his client after all. And call the *Times* while you're at it and give your pal over there the story. I'm sure he'll appreciate having today's headline confirmed by the owner of the station."

As his words echoed off the walls, he moved purposefully toward the door, his back stiff and straight. Kelly, who'd been immobilized by a scene she felt powerless to stop, jumped to her feet and went after him.

"Grant, wait!" she pleaded. "I know you're angry and rightfully so, but don't throw away everything you've worked for without taking the time to sit down and think things through."

He shook his head. "There's nothing to think about," he insisted determinedly.

"Of course there is," she argued. But it was useless. He had already stormed through the outer office, nearly knocking over a man waiting there in his haste. The man looked from Grant to Kelly and a speculative gleam lit his eyes. Before he could say a word, though, Kelly slammed the door and turned back to a stunned Lyndon Phillips.

"You know something, Mr. Phillips?" she said, her voice slashing at him like the sharp crack of a whip. "For a man who's supposed to be so smart, sometimes you act like a bloody fool!"

CHAPTER EIGHT

Kelly was just about to elaborate on her remark to Lyndon when Janie slipped into the room, motioning frantically for her to lower her voice. Kelly sighed.

"What is it now?" she asked wearily.

"That man outside, the one Mr. Andrews bumped into, he's Dean Evans."

At Kelly's blank expression the secretary said, "From the *Times.* He can hear every word you're saying in here."

"Oh, my God," Kelly swore softly. "Get him out of here, Janie."

"But you have an appointment with him. Remember, Tom set it up right after you started here."

"You'll have to see him, Kelly," Lyndon said insistently. "If you back out now, he'll tear you apart in tomorrow's paper. He's probably got enough material right now for one helluva lead paragraph."

The image of Grant's angry departure flashed through Kelly's mind and she knew her boss was right. She would have to see Dean Evans, but she would see him alone. She didn't need Lyndon on hand to make matters even worse than they already were. This time, if there were any foul-ups, she'd be responsible.

"Okay," she agreed at last. "Give me five minutes or so, Janie, and then send him in."

"What're you plannin' on sayin' to him?" Lyndon asked.

"I'll think of something," she told him with far more assurance than she felt. "But I don't want you hanging around to watch. I want to handle this one on my own."

"Kelly, girl, I know these guys. They can eat you alive. Maybe I ought to stay here and help."

Kelly's smile was rueful, her tone only mildly critical as she said, "I'd say you've already done more than your share. Now it's my turn."

"Okay," he agreed reluctantly just as Janie ushered the reporter into the office. Lyndon greeted him effusively, then introduced him to Kelly before excusing himself. "I'd like to stay and chat with you, son, but I've got some business to attend to. You and Kelly here can get to know each other without me buttin' in."

He winked and lowered his voice to a conspiratorial whisper. "You listen to what she tells you. She knows a heckuva lot more about this business than I do, but don't you go tellin' her I said that."

Then he was gone and Kelly was alone with the man whose acerbic comments in the morning paper had virtually destroyed the station's negotiations with Grant. During an extended silence they studied each other, measuring each other, trying to spot potential weaknesses. Dean Evans was the first to speak.

"How are the negotiations with Grant Andrews moving along?" he asked.

"Why don't you tell me?" Kelly suggested. "You seem to have some inside information."

"Was there anything inaccurate about that column?" he parried.

"Everything but the spelling of our names. But I'm sure you're not interested or you would have sought out the actual facts before you wrote it," she said calmly, not allowing her voice to betray the anger she felt toward him. She noted that for just a fraction of a second he looked uncomfortable. Her jab had apparently landed right on his professional ego. "I'll have my secretary bring you a copy of the statement we issued this morning. It should help to clear up any misunderstanding."

"I saw Mr. Andrews leaving here as I came in. Judging from his expression, I'd have to guess that your contract talks aren't going too well."

"Your guessing games have led you pretty far afield already, Mr. Evans, but feel free to continue playing them. Our talks with Mr. Andrews are continuing and I have no intention of discussing their substance with you or anyone else until we have reached an agreement."

"But do you expect to reach one?" he persisted.

"Mr. Evans," Kelly said patiently, "that subject is closed. This interview was arranged so that we could talk about my plans for this station. If you wish to discuss that, fine. If not, I have work to do."

In the face of her determination, Dean Evans backed down. For the next hour he limited his questions to issues of programing, expansion of the news operation, and her commitment to the creation of educational shows for children. The last was one of her favorite themes, and she talked enthusiastically about the need for local stations to take responsibility for the sort of programing they offered youngsters.

"I'm not talking about just what adults think kids should watch. I'd like to have the kids themselves involved in planning the shows. I'm convinced you can offer something on Saturday morning that's more meaningful than cartoons, yet is fun at the same time," she concluded. Dean Evans nodded in agreement and turned off his tape recorder.

"Thanks, Miss Patrick," he said sincerely. "I appreciate your taking the time to see me."

"Certainly," Kelly said politely, walking with him to the door. Just as he was about to leave, he turned back to her and Kelly suddenly detected a malicious gleam in his eyes.

"One last question, Miss Patrick," he requested. "Are you and Grant Andrews having an affair?"

Stunned by the unexpectedness of the question and by its damaging implications, Kelly fought to keep her eyes level with his. "I'm not sure what sort of story you're after, Mr. Evans," she responded forcefully, "but I won't dignify that question with a response."

He shrugged. "Suit yourself," he said smugly. "I can always find another source for confirmation."

"Unless you're referring to Mr. Andrews, I can't think of another soul who could give you the sort of confirmation you need. I doubt you'll have much luck with him," she replied, barely restraining her mounting fury. "I'd also suggest you have a talk with your paper's attorneys about the laws on libel. I think you'll find them enlightening."

With that, she firmly shut the door to her office in his face. Walking slowly back to her desk, she tried to still the angry pounding of her heart by taking deep breaths. If Dean Evans's parting shot had been any indication, tomorrow's column was going to be filled with even more lies and distortions than today's.

Ironically, she thought in retrospect, she had actually felt in control of the interview for a few brief moments. She should have known better. She knew the man's reputation. He went for the jugular. Despite her warning about libel, she knew he would write what he pleased. His readers, of course, would love it.

Even knowing what to expect didn't prepare Kelly for the feelings that swept through her the next morning as she read Dean Evans's column. He'd written nothing about their interview at all. Instead, he had portrayed a station being torn apart by a rift between management and the town's top anchorman. As she had feared he would, he had used the accidental meeting with Grant in her outer office to spin a tale of bitter infighting and imminent firings.

"But, of course," he had written sarcastically, "there could be another explanation for the scene I witnessed in station manager Kelly Patrick's office yesterday afternoon. Rumors have been circulating for days that the sparks between her and anchorman Andrews aren't all based on their professional differences.

"Miss Patrick declined to comment on the speculation about a liaison with the newsman, but it's beginning to appear that the romantic intrigue at this station could rival anything on the daytime soaps or even prime-time's seamier *Dallas* or *Dynasty*. Stay tuned. . . ."

Kelly's hands were shaking as she dropped the paper on the floor. She reached for the cup of coffee on the table beside her and, using both hands to steady it, brought it to her lips. The steaming black liquid burned her tongue, but at least it distracted her momentarily from the other, more devastating pain she had felt at seeing her private life bared before the entire city. She had built up an immunity to the professional attacks by television critics, but this was something new and it hurt.

After several minutes the hard knot that had formed in the pit of her stomach began to ease. In its place a healthy rage was born and she swore she would find a way to get even with Dean Evans. She would force him to retract every vicious word he had written. Oh, it was true enough that she was having an affair with Grant—if you could call one all-too-brief evening an affair. But their relationship had nothing to do with what was happening at the station and it certainly was no one else's business. In a courtroom it would have been declared irrelevant.

Or would it, she wondered. Realistically, no matter how much she might wish it were otherwise, perhaps it was impossible to separate her very personal feelings for Grant from their business ties. Certainly they seemed to keep getting in the way despite their best intentions. As she examined the issue from every angle, like a photographer studying the lighting for a picture, the doorbell rang.

Pulling her robe more securely around her and running her fingers through her hair, she crossed the room and called out, "Who is it?"

"Grant." The reply was abrupt and harsh. Judging from the tone, this would be another bitter, accusatory encounter. Kelly wasn't sure she could take that at this hour of the morning. Still, as Grant's pounding rattled the door, she knew there was no way around it. She might as well let him in and get it over with.

Forcing a smile to her lips, she opened the door. "My, you're certainly out early today," she said brightly. "What's up?"

"You know perfectly well what's up," he said, waving the paper in her face. "This . . . this piece of trash."

Kelly's façade nearly crumbled, but she managed

a flip retort. "Charming, wasn't it? Think we should sue?"

"On what grounds?" Grant countered. "Unfortunately, most of what he's written is true. He's just twisted it a bit here and there to make it more sensational. What I want to know is how the hell he found out about us?"

"Well, he didn't find out from me, if that's what you're wondering."

"He was in your office yesterday afternoon," Grant stated flatly.

"Yes. And he was definitely on a fishing expedition, until I told him I wouldn't answer any questions related to our negotiations. Then, as he was leaving, he tossed out his bombshell. He asked me point blank if you and I were having an affair."

"And you said?"

Kelly threw up her hands in disgust and stalked across the room. Turning to face Grant, she snapped, "What the hell do you think I said? I told him it was none of his damn business."

"Obviously, he took that as a confirmation."

"Obviously," she agreed sarcastically.

Suddenly the expression in Grant's eyes softened. He sighed and ran his fingers through his already unruly hair. "I'm sorry, Kelly," he apologized. "This has been rough on you, hasn't it?"

The unexpected turnaround in his attitude, the sympathy she heard in his voice, took Kelly by surprise. She met his gaze and for a moment the tough veneer that enabled her to cope almost cracked. She gave him a wry smile. "Well, this is not exactly what I call a great start to the day," she said in what was a massive understatement.

"Kelly," he said softly, taking a single step toward her and holding out his arms. She hesitated briefly before moving into his embrace, needing the strength and comfort she knew she would find there. They remained together, their bodies pressed close, their hearts beating almost in unison for several minutes before Grant spoke again.

"I really am sorry about this," he whispered, his breath a warm, lightly teasing breeze against her neck. "I've been so angry about the whole mess that I never stopped to think about what it must be doing to you. I'm used to having my personal life splashed all over the gossip columns in town. I still hate it, but after a while you get so you can accept the fiction along with the fact and ignore all of it."

"I'm afraid I'm not quite that sophisticated. I'd like to put the screws to Mr. Dean Evans, ace reporter, and hang him out to dry on the evening news."

Grant chuckled at her defiance. "You believe in the 'don't get mad, get even' philosophy?"

"Absolutely."

"Forget it, boss lady," he said, stroking her loose hair back from her brow. "In this business that never pays. Fighting back, unless you've been seriously libeled, only prolongs the issue and keeps it in print where the public can wallow in every gory detail."

"There is one sure way to put an end to all the speculation," Kelly suggested.

"What's that?"

"You could sign your contract," she said softly, gambling that Grant wanted to stop the public feuding as badly as she did and that he would see the logic behind the suggestion. Almost instantly, though, his hold on her stiffened for instant and then she knew she had miscalculated. Grant dropped his arms from around her, his features frozen into the hard, cold mask she'd come to recognize as the predecessor to an explosion of anger.

"So," he said bitterly, "this *was* just another move in the game you and Lyndon have been playing. And to think I was actually prepared to feel sorry for you. I should have known you were far too tough to let a little thing like having your personal life written about in the newspapers bother you. God, what an actress you are!"

Kelly winced at the pain and rage she heard in his voice. "You're wrong," she swore softly, trying to counteract the damage she had done with her poorly timed suggestion. She reached out to touch him, but allowed her hand to drop when she saw him withdraw from the contact. "I only thought if you would sign, we could end all of this before it destroys . . . before it destroys everything."

"Everything, meaning your career?"

"Everything, meaning us," she corrected hotly. She felt for a moment as if she were going to cry, her vision suddenly blurred by tears. But she refused to break down, to lose control at such a crucial moment. Grant would probably suspect her of using tears as a sympathy tactic anyway. Argue first, cry on your own time, she coached herself.

He studied her intently. "Are you telling me that our relationship is the only thing that matters to you?" he asked quietly.

Sensing a trap, Kelly said firmly, "Yes."

"Then step aside and let someone else handle the contract talks. Turn them over to Lyndon. He's running them anyway."

She shook her head slowly. "I can't do that. I have to see this through. It's my responsibility."

"And I have a responsibility as well. To myself. I can't sign this contract now, Kelly. If I do, you and Lyndon will have won."

"Won what? This isn't a contest. It's a business deal."

"That's what it should be," he agreed. "But our feelings have turned it into something else. You and I will never be able to work this out, not with Lyndon on hand to put a scheme behind your every move. And you're right. In the end it may destroy us."

"Are you willing to risk that?"

"I have no choice," he said flatly.

"Why not? Is your fierce male pride at stake? Are you willing to give up a career you love just to make a point?"

"Perhaps," he said slowly, as though examining the possibility for the first time. "Perhaps pride—and principles—are the only things that are important in the end."

"Not love?"

"Love shouldn't be a contradiction. In our case it seems to be and that's what I can't accept."

Kelly shook her head as if to clear it of the confusing thoughts that tumbled about. "I just don't understand you, Grant. This might make sense if Lyndon and I were trying to cheat you, but we're not. The contract is more than generous and you know it."

"Let's just say I'm not wild about your tactics," he told her, his tone mildly rebuking.

"You've made that plain enough. So," she wondered, "what now?"

Grant was silent for some time, his face reflecting the painful questions to which they still needed to find answers. "I don't know," he said simply, looking at her helplessly. "Why don't we spend the rest of the day together and see if we can figure out where we go from here?"

More than anything, Kelly wanted to do just that, but the contract stood between them like some sort of insurmountable barrier. For a piece of paper, it had an amazing amount of strength, the strength to keep two people apart. Until it was signed, it was pointless for them to try to work out their other differences.

"Okay," she agreed. "We'll spend the day together . . . after we've negotiated your new contract. We're not leaving this room until we've gone over it clause by clause and settled this once and for all."

"I'm perfectly willing to stay locked in here with you all day," Grant agreed with a wicked grin. "But

I can't promise to keep my mind on the bargaining table."

Kelly's breath caught in her throat as his words stirred the memory of another day the two of them had spent together. Had it been only a week ago? So much had happened since then and it seemed it would be impossible to recapture the rapport they had shared. Besides, making love with Grant would only cloud their situation further now. Knowing that, though, did not stop a dull ache from spreading through her, an ache that could only be soothed with his touch.

"Forget it," she told him briskly, willing her body to ignore the warm nearness of the man who was capable of leading her to a dangerous new precipice of sensations. "I've changed my mind. If we're going to spend the day together, it won't be in this room."

Grant sighed wistfully. "I had a feeling you were going to say that. Go and get dressed and I'll take you someplace . . ."

"Public," Kelly suggested.

"If you insist."

"I do."

He moved to within inches of her. Reaching out, he trailed a finger lightly down the side of her neck, then over the silky material of her robe until it came to rest on her breast. Gently, he traced the outline of the nipple as it stood out firmly against the thin material. Kelly's body trembled as an undeniable hunger for a more intense, thorough contact coursed through her.

"You sure?" he asked softly.

"Yes," she said shakily.

As though satisfied with the response he had elicited from her, Grant moved away. "Sometimes the price of holding on to one's principles is awfully high, isn't it?"

Not trusting herself to speak, Kelly nodded, knowing now, in some small way, the anguish he was going through. With that knowledge came the conviction that somehow they would work through their problems. They had to.

CHAPTER NINE

As Kelly showered and dressed, she began having doubts about spending the day with Grant. What if they were seen together? It would only substantiate what Dean Evans had written about a romance between them. She hated the thought of having more innuendos about her private life bared for public scrutiny. It made her relationship with Grant seem tawdry and sordid, as though it were nothing more than the standard grist for the Chicago gossip mill.

And yet, she reasoned, what additional harm could possibly result from the two of them spending an innocent afternoon in a public place? Any damage to their reputations or careers had already been done. As for the way such publicity made her feel, she would have to learn to take it in stride, just as she had the columns criticizing her professional decisions.

Her mind made up at last, she returned to the living room, where Grant had settled himself on the sofa and was lost in the sports section. Not really wanting to interrupt him, but wanting to be at least on the edge of his consciousness, Kelly went and perched beside him on the arm of the sofa. When she rested her hand lightly on his shoulder, he smiled slightly but gave no other indication that he was aware of her presence.

Spurred on to a more daring approach by his apparent lack of interest, she ran her fingers through the thick hair that curled along the back of his neck. Her hand lingered on his warm skin, gently massaging it until she heard his sharp intake of breath. It was the only sign he gave that she was having any effect on him at all. At the same time her own pulse was beating rapidly as a pleasant warmth stole through her. It was all she could do to restrain herself from pursuing a more intimate exploration. Her desire for Grant was an almost tangible thing. His power over her body was an exciting, yet frightening, sensation. Considering his seeming ability to ignore her as he was right now, she wasn't at all sure she liked the sensation.

"Is the news that interesting?" she asked at last.

"Not particularly," he admitted, looking up at her and reaching out to put an arm around her waist. "In fact, I haven't been able to get through a complete sentence for the last ten minutes."

"Then why haven't you said anything?"

He grinned. "I wanted to see how far you'd go to get my attention."

"You rat!" she said, escaping his embrace and facing him indignantly. "You are definitely no gentleman."

"And you, love, certainly were not behaving like

a lady," he teased. "Don't worry though. I promise not to hold it against you that you seem to have turned into a wanton woman."

"If that's what I've become, I have only you to blame," she retorted, trying not to return his grin.

"I can live with that," he told her. "Now, do we get out of here or shall we stay and see exactly how wanton I've made you?"

"We go," Kelly said firmly, heading for the door. "I think you've done enough tampering with my personality for one day."

"Your personality was the last thing on my mind," Grant responded, giving her a broad wink. Kelly made a face at him. "Okay. Okay," he said resignedly. "Let's go."

The bantering continued as Grant drove toward downtown. When he pulled into a parking lot near the lake, Kelly gave him a questioning glance. "I'm taking you to Chicagofest," he said in response to her unasked question.

A feeling of panic rushed over Kelly. "Grant, do you think that's such a good idea? People are bound to recognize you. You won't have a minute's peace."

"Sometimes the best place to be alone is in the middle of a crowd," he said. "You'll see. It'll be just fine."

Reluctantly, Kelly followed him toward the entrance to Navy Pier, where the annual Chicagofest extravaganza of music, food, and crafts was held. Grant bought their tickets and they joined the large throng of people already milling around the various booths.

"Hungry?" Grant inquired. Kelly sniffed the air, which was filled with the scent of Italian, Chinese, and American food, and nodded. She'd never been able to resist the temptations offered by these outdoor vendors. "Breakfast or lunch?" Grant asked.

"Breakfast?"

"Sure. What's better for breakfast than a sugary fried doughnut and a cup of coffee?"

Kelly's mouth watered at the thought of it. Still, she frowned. "It sounds disgustingly fattening. Where do we get some?" she added with a grin.

"Just up ahead. You grab one of those tables over there and I'll get it and bring it back."

He soon returned with a white paper bag full of sticky, sweet pastry and cups of steaming coffee, and they stuffed themselves contentedly while looking over a schedule for the various music pavilions. Kelly couldn't get over the number and variety of performances. "This is incredible!" she marveled. There were rock, blues, jazz, and country-western shows virtually every hour through the afternoon and evening. That night there would be a performance by Aretha Franklin on the main stage as well. And it was all for the single admission price. It was, by far, the best entertainment bargain she'd ever seen.

"What first?" Grant wanted to know.

"You decide," she insisted. "I can't make up my

mind when there are this many choices. I want to see it all."

"We will before the day is over," he promised. Checking his watch, he noted, "It's just about time for the next jazz performance. Let's go hear that and then we can walk around for a while and check out the booths."

For the next half-hour they sat in the warm sun while a local jazz group filled the air with a soaring sound that was a taunting reminder of the man next to Kelly, his hard thigh pressed against hers. She tried to concentrate on the music, but her body seemed only attuned to the nearness of Grant. Stealing a look at him, her eyes met his and they shared a knowing smile that told her he, too, was having difficulty keeping his attention on the performance. When it was over, he silently took her hand and led her along the perimeter of the pier, past the other music stages.

By now Kelly was beginning to relax. Grant had been right about the crowd. While many people recognized him, they were far too intent on their own fun to intrude on his. There were occasional smiles or greetings, but nothing more. Certainly no one seemed especially interested in the identity of his companion.

There was one nervous moment when they suddenly came upon the station's booth. Kelly had forgotten it would be there. Tom Winston had told her about it, of course, but the plans had been completed long before her arrival and she hadn't really thought about it since their one brief conversation.

"Shouldn't we stop?" she asked as Grant steered her away.

"I don't think that would be a good idea under the circumstances," he said.

"You're probably right," she agreed reluctantly. "But what if they saw us? Won't they think it odd that we didn't stop?"

"Maybe. But I'd rather risk that than drop by and know that they'll start speculating the minute we're gone about what we're doing here together," he insisted.

The decision made, Kelly tried to push the incident from her mind as the afternoon wore on. It wasn't difficult. There were so many things to do and see and Grant seemed intent on making sure they didn't miss any of them. They watched skydivers plunge through the cloudless sky over the lake, laughed as a mime wandered through the crowd imitating those he saw, listened to more music, snacked on slices of thick pizza, egg rolls, and spinach pie, and stopped at every craft booth. They were talking with a young jeweler at one of the stalls, when Kelly saw an intricate gold ring the man had designed. It was delicate and unique and she fell instantly in love with it. Although it was new, it reminded her of the design of the antique locket she always wore.

"I think the lady would like to try on the ring," Grant told the young man.

"No, really, it isn't necessary," she said. "It's lovely, but . . ."

"But nothing. You like it, don't you?" Grant argued.

"Yes."

"Then let's see if it fits," he said, taking it from the jeweler. Holding Kelly's right hand firmly in his, he slipped the ring on the third finger. It fit perfectly. "We'll take it," he said firmly, refusing to allow her to take it off.

When they had walked on, Kelly tried again to remove the ring. "I can't accept it," she told him.

"Why not? You know what you pay me. You know I can afford it."

"That's not the point."

"Then exactly what is the point?" he asked impatiently. "Kelly, I want to give it to you. I like the way your eyes sparkle when you look at it. Like a little girl on Christmas morning. Don't deny me the pleasure of seeing that sparkle."

"Oh, Grant," she said softly, her gaze meeting his. "How can I possibly say no when you put it like that?"

"I'm hoping you can't," he admitted, reaching out to gently stroke her cheek. "So, what's the verdict?"

She stood on tiptoe and kissed him lightly. "Thank you, Santa."

"You're welcome," he said with a deep laugh, draping an arm around her shoulders and squeezing them. "Now let's go find a shady spot to sit for

Aretha Franklin's performance. I don't think I can walk another step."

"Don't tell me all this activity has been too much for you," Kelly teased.

"Of course it has been. I'm used to spending Saturday stretched out on the sofa in front of the TV watching the Cubs or the White Sox. You've had me on my feet all day for two weeks in a row now."

"You weren't on your feet *all* that time, as I recall," she countered with a wicked gleam in her eyes. "Besides, I'd try to be sympathetic, but I suspect the exercise is good for you."

"Let me guess. You want me to be in shape for my annual physical."

"Exactly," Kelly agreed. "I don't want to have to fork out higher insurance premiums for you on top of all the other perks in your contract."

"Careful," he warned, though there was a devilish gleam in his eye, "or I'll remind you that unless you play your cards right, there won't be a contract to worry about."

Kelly grimaced. "Forget I brought it up."

He nodded. "Good thinking." He stopped then and looked around. "How's this?" he asked, gesturing toward a patch of grass that, for the moment anyway, was uncrowded and had a large oak tree shading it from the rapidly sinking sun.

"Perfect," she said, sinking down gratefully on the cool grass. "There's only one small problem."

"What's that?"

"We can't see the stage from here."

"That's not a problem. That's reality. I refuse to sit on one of those hard benches in the middle of that mob in order to *see* Aretha Franklin. Here we can be comfortable and hear her. That'll have to do," he said, stretching out beside her.

"You know, Mr. Andrews," she said as if making a sudden discovery, "you have an incredibly dictatorial side to your nature."

"I know," he murmured happily, as though she'd paid him a great compliment. "So do you. That's what makes this relationship of ours so interesting."

"Grant Andrews, I am not dictatorial!" Kelly replied heatedly. "Ask anyone at the station. I believe in participatory management."

"Sure," he agreed, grinning up at her. "As long as you get your own way in the end."

"That's not true!"

"Isn't it? You've made a great show of negotiating my new contract, but I can't seem to recall your changing a single clause once you'd settled on the terms in your own mind."

"That's because you haven't asked for any specific changes," she argued. "I'll listen to any reasonable request you have."

"Define reasonable," he countered. "Is that something that meets your standards of acceptability or mine?"

"If we're negotiating, it should be agreeable to both of us. We both may have to bend a little."

"Remember that when talks resume, boss lady," he said lightly.

"Since we're already on the subject, we could resume them right now," Kelly suggested.

"And spoil a perfectly beautiful evening? Not a chance. Any negotiations we conduct from now on will be held in a far more businesslike atmosphere than this. My God, there's a full moon up there, soft music will begin any moment, and I'm exhausted. You could probably talk me into almost anything."

"Really?" Kelly said softly, leaning down to brush a kiss across his lips. "What exactly would I have to do?"

"Just keep that up," he murmured, pulling her down beside him. Breathlessly, she touched her lips to his again, but this time there was no retreat. Grant held her firmly against him, his mouth warm and moist against hers as his tongue teased and probed, seeking entrance beyond her lips.

When, at last, he released her, Kelly asked shakily, "Don't you think we're a little old to be necking in a public place?"

"What does age have to do with it?" Grant replied. "Look around. We're hardly alone."

Glancing about, Kelly saw that he was right. Couples all around them were clinging together in the soft night air, seduced by the starry sky and the romantic music that was now drifting over them from the loudspeakers at the main stage. Although the songs being sung by Aretha Franklin warned of loves lost, her audience seemed oblivious of the message. Clearly, they believed the night's magical moments were forever. Kelly wanted to believe that too, but common sense told her that there were many things that could yet go wrong with her relationship with Grant. The thought scared her, so when Grant pulled her back into the circle of his arms, she clung to him.

As though he sensed her fear, Grant held her more tightly. "What is it, Kelly? You're trembling."

"I'm just a little chilly, I guess," she told him, thankful that he didn't point out that it was eighty degrees and humid. She knew only that she couldn't admit the truth to him, that she couldn't reveal that she was afraid of losing him.

Suddenly she knew that she wanted to be alone with Grant. She needed to have him make love to her, to show her as only he could that she was more than a successful executive, that she was a woman who could be cherished and desired. Only Grant seemed capable of fusing those two very different aspects of her being into a whole person. Any feminist worth her salt would have a fit, Kelly thought with a smile. Well, too bad. She had proven she could make it alone. But she was tired of being alone.

Strength and independence were wonderful qualities. They enabled Kelly to survive when the going was rough. But there was nothing wrong with wanting another person to share your life, with loving someone who enriched your life merely by being a part of it. Meeting Grant had shown her that. For the first time Kelly felt she was willing to compromise and to relinquish some of that independence on which she'd prided herself for so long.

Curving her body so that it fit perfectly into the hard contours of Grant's, she ran her hands over his shoulders and along his muscular arms.

"Change your mind about necking in public?" he inquired lightly.

"Actually I was thinking we ought to go someplace a little more private," she suggested brazenly, her eyes meeting his and igniting a blaze of passion. "What do you think?"

"I think you've hit on the one idea that could make me move from this spot," Grant said, giving her a hard, breathtaking kiss before getting to his feet and helping her up.

Grant brushed the grass from her sundress and from her bare shoulders, lingering for a moment on the sensitive nape of her neck. Kelly's lips parted as she gazed up at him and he seemed about to bend and kiss her. Instead, though, he linked her arm through his and led her across the grass, careful to avoid the couples scattered through the shadows.

"I feel as though I'm walking through a minefield," Kelly said with a giggle.

"I suppose it's similar. I can just imagine the explosion if you happened to ruin somebody's romantic mood."

They strolled on, arm in arm, stopping just once to watch a child's pink, helium-filled balloon escape and fly crazily through the dark sky. The toddler was crying lustily as his frantic parents tried to distract him from the balloon that was floating farther and farther away.

When Kelly and Grant neared the gate, she paused and looked back, unaware of the sad expression that flitted across her face.

"Is something wrong?" Grant asked, his eyes watching her with a puzzled look.

"It's been such a perfect day. I guess a part of me just doesn't want it to end."

"The day's not over yet," Grant assured her softly. He leaned down to kiss her. "Not by a long shot."

Kelly's arms crept up and around his neck and she molded herself into him. Her senses reeled from the surge of longing that washed over her as she clung to Grant, her lips meeting his in a bruising kiss that held nothing back.

Then, suddenly, the night seemed to explode with light around them. As though from a great distance, Kelly heard voices calling out Grant's name and then her own. When she would have broken away from his embrace, he held her head against his chest and ordered her to stay still.

"All right, fellas, that's enough. You got what you were after. I'm sure your editors will be pleased," he said sarcastically to the handful of photographers who remained poised and ready to snatch another shot of the anchorman and his current lover. When Kelly realized what had happened, she twisted out of Grant's arms and faced the men indignantly.

"Don't you all have anything better to do than invade our privacy?" she snapped.

"Lady, if you want privacy, stay at home," one brash young man with a beard retorted, snapping another picture of Kelly, her lips sensuously swollen and her hair mussed. It was evident that Grant was the man responsible for her disarray, and the photographer wasn't about to miss a chance to catch the couple in such a revealing pose.

Kelly wanted to grab the camera from the man's hands and smash it to the ground, but when she took a step in his direction, Grant held her back.

"Forget it, honey. It won't help," he warned her. "Let's just get out of here."

Mustering every ounce of pride she could manage, Kelly strode past the photographers, her head held high. But when they reached the car, she stood trembling with a rage she couldn't control. "How dare they!" she demanded, facing Grant angrily. "What right do they have to sneak up on us and take those pictures and then print them?"

"They're just doing their jobs," Grant told her wearily. "Unfortunately, their readers love that sort of thing. Editors can't get enough of it. They figure it sells papers. Just be thankful we're not national celebrities; we'd be in every supermarket in the country by next week."

"The thought that our picture will be plastered across every paper in Chicago by tomorrow morning isn't very comforting," she insisted.

"Not very," he admitted. "I'm sorry, Kelly. I knew we were taking a risk coming here, but I thought it would be okay."

She heard the sincerity in his voice and saw the

brief flash of pain in his eyes. "It was okay. It was more than okay . . . it was perfect until the very end."

"I don't suppose you could just pretend that last kiss made you see fireworks," he suggested hopefully.

"I might be able to manage that," she said, reaching up to brush a strand of hair from his forehead. Her fingers drifted across his lips, tracing the outline of his mouth. The anger that had left her warm and shaking only moments before melted away and was replaced by another type of warmth entirely. Despite everything, she still wanted Grant with every fiber of her body.

"Let's go home now," she whispered huskily. "Tomorrow will just have to take care of itself."

CHAPTER TEN

When Kelly walked into the station on Monday morning she faced an uncomfortable wall of silence. Conversations halted when she entered a room. Her staff greeted her nervously, then gratefully escaped as quickly as possible. No one mentioned the pictures in the Sunday papers, at least in front of her, but she knew that everyone had seen them. She could tell by their awkward behavior, by the look of condemnation in their eyes. Those who'd disliked her from the outset were gloating over what they viewed as her public humiliation. Her supporters obviously thought she had made a terrible mistake and they seemed puzzled and disillusioned by her behavior.

After enduring an entire morning of whispered gossip in the corridors and silence in her presence, Kelly called Janie into her office.

"Yes, Miss Patrick," the girl said, unable to look her boss in the eye.

"I want you to get the management staff in here for a meeting in fifteen minutes. Hold all of my calls until after that meeting," she instructed.

"But you have an appointment with Grant Andrews's agent in a few minutes," Janie reminded her.

"He can wait. The meeting won't take long and it's too important to be put off any longer. I should have called it first thing this morning."

When Janie left, Kelly took a deep breath and tried to think of something she could say that would improve the situation. She had been gaining ground with the staff and now she was about to lose it all because of this ridiculous incident. She knew she couldn't allow things to deteriorate to the point that she lost their respect.

Fortunately, the weekend seemed to have smoothed out her relationship with Grant. He had been wonderfully warm and supportive on Sunday morning when they had skimmed through the papers together in search of the photographs taken at Chicagofest. He had reassured her that people would forget quickly, as soon as the papers provided them with a new scandal, a new bit of titillating gossip. She drew strength from his reassurances as she prepared for this meeting.

When everyone had assembled in her office, Kelly faced them directly and said softly, "I think there are some issues we need to clear up." Her voice was calm, but her hands were clenched tightly together in her lap, out of sight of her audience.

"As you all are obviously aware, several photographers caught Mr. Andrews and me in what might be construed as a compromising position. I am not proud of that. I'm also sorry that this has resulted in some rather unseemly publicity for the station. However, those pictures do not change the fact that I am still running this television station and that I need your support to do that . . . now more than ever.

"If we are to keep this incident from costing us a great deal, we will need to present a united front to our competitors and to the community. The press has been hovering around this station like a school of piranhas. If anyone senses that there is a rift in our management team, they will use the slightest rumor to destroy our standing in the market. If you want to speculate about my relationship with Mr. Andrews privately, I can't stop you. If you do it publicly, you'll be fired. Is that clear?"

Looks of shocked disbelief followed her harsh edict, but slowly everyone in the room nodded assent. "Thank you," Kelly said quietly. "Any questions before we all get back to work?"

For several seconds no one spoke, then one of the salesmen broke the silence. "I guess I'll ask this for everybody: Are we going to be able to hold on to Grant Andrews after this?"

Each of the men and women in the room faced her expectantly. A good deal hinged on her reply, and they all knew it. Kelly knew she had to be honest with them.

"I have a meeting with Mr. Andrews's agent as soon as we're finished up here. I hope to be able to conclude our negotiations quickly and that the results will be positive." The faces around her brightened at her words, but she quickly tempered her optimism. "However, I must be candid with you. The reports in the papers over the last few days, and now yesterday's photographs, haven't helped. Mr. Andrews feels, and rightly so, that we have done him a disservice by publicizing the possibility that we have another candidate for his position. I'm going to have to convince him and his agent that the only anchorman we're interested in having here is Grant Andrews."

"*You* certainly ought to be able to convince him of anything you want to," a woman from the programming department said spitefully.

Kelly ignored the sarcasm and said only, "Unless there are more questions, this meeting is concluded. I don't want to keep Mr. Andrews's agent waiting any longer than I have to."

As the others left, John Marshall paused by Kelly's desk. "Good luck, kiddo. Just remember that Kent Hastings is Grant's *agent.* He may not like it, but Grant will make the final decision about whether or not to sign a new contract. You think about what you need to do to get Grant to do that and don't let Hastings intimidate you."

"I can't afford to let him intimidate me," Kelly said, giving John Marshall a weak grin. "So I'll just have to intimidate him first."

The news director returned her smile. "I'd like to stick around for that."

"No way. I'm much braver without an audience. I'll call you after the meeting and let you know how it went."

"Okay," he agreed ruefully. "I guess I can wait a couple of hours."

As he walked out the door Kelly called after him, "You might keep your fingers crossed while you're waiting."

"Sure thing."

Kelly buzzed for Janie. "Are Mr. Hastings and Mr. Andrews here yet?"

"Mr. Hastings is here alone. I don't think Mr. Andrews is coming," the secretary said.

That bit of information threw Kelly slightly. She'd been counting on Grant's presence to get her through this meeting successfully. She thought she knew how to reach him now, what it would take to win him over. If Kent Hastings insisted on keeping Grant away from the negotiations, her job would be much tougher. Contract talks always were when a buffer kept the two principals apart. Sighing, she told Janie, "Then I suppose you should send Mr. Hastings on in."

Kent Hastings was almost exactly as Kelly had pictured him. He was tall and trim in his three-piece gray suit. He appeared to be about fifty, though there were only a few telltale wrinkles on his tanned face and a few strands of gray hair at his temples. His eyes were a penetrating blue and his handshake was firm.

"Miss Patrick, it's a pleasure to meet you at last," he said smoothly.

"Mr. Hastings, won't you sit down?" Kelly said, gesturing toward a chair opposite her desk. She was not taken in by the agent's superficial charm. He was like a wolf who'd lure you into his lair and then attack when you least expected it. She couldn't allow him that opportunity. She had to take the initiative from the start and hang on to it. "I'm sure Mr. Andrews has given you a copy of the contract we've offered him. Mr. Phillips and I are very aware of your client's value to this station and we've tried to acknowledge his contributions with an offer that is more than fair. I assume you've advised him to accept it."

"As a matter of fact, I've advised him to begin looking elsewhere," the agent said flatly. "I do not think it is in his best interest to remain with an organization that seems intent on subjecting him to public ridicule."

"This station has done *nothing* to damage your client's reputation in this town. In fact, it is his reputation that has encouraged the media to pounce on this story with such avid interest. I should think you'd be pleased that so many people care whether he stays with us."

"Oh, I'm pleased about that all right. In fact, it proves to me that my client's future would be better served by taking advantage of that interest to move on. His audience will follow him."

"I'm sure it would—initially," Kelly conceded. "However, Mr. Hastings, this station made Grant Andrews into a journalistic superstar in this town. It can do the same for his replacement."

"No one *made* Grant Andrews a superstar, my dear. He has a unique combination of talents that, if anything, made this station's news department a success. I suggest you not forget that."

"We aren't likely to get anywhere by trading barbs," Kelly said, changing tactics. "Why don't you just tell me what it is that Mr. Andrews would like? I'm sure we can come to some agreement that will prove mutually beneficial."

Kent Hastings named a figure thousands of dollars above Kelly's original offer. Although she knew she had allowed herself room to bargain with that offer, she cringed inwardly at the thought of trying to get Lyndon to agree to Grant's demand. Still, she continued to meet the agent's gaze calmly. "What else?" she asked.

"The new contract will be for ten years, with appropriate escalation clauses," he said as casually as if he'd asked for a mere coffeepot to be installed in Grant's office.

"That's unheard of!" Kelly said indignantly. "No one will grant a ten-year contract in this business, and you know it!"

"They will if they want Grant Andrews," he insisted flatly.

"What else?" Kelly asked, her stomach beginning to churn.

"There are a few other minor items, but they're all spelled out in this draft I've prepared for you. Why don't you look it over at your leisure and I'll call you tomorrow."

"That'll be fine, Mr. Hastings," she agreed, though she dreaded the thought of trying to prepare a solid counteroffer in less than twenty-four hours. She would do it, though, if she had to stay up all night. Kent Hastings might think he had the upper hand, but she had learned a few tricks about bargaining herself and she would use every one of them.

Kelly walked the agent to the door, engaging in small talk even as her mind began to race on to the task ahead of her. Holding out her hand, she told him, "I'll be waiting for your call."

Although he clasped her hand firmly, Kelly noticed that he seemed uncomfortable. Suddenly she realized with some surprise that Kent Hastings was not used to dealing with women in a business setting. It was a fact to be filed away for later use.

"By the way, Miss Patrick, there's one thing I'm going to have to insist on until this contract matter is settled."

"Oh? What's that?"

"I want you to stay away from my client unless there is some sort of routine business about which you must communicate with him directly. Any other communication I expect to go through me."

"I understand," she said, wondering whether Grant was aware of this impending separation. She recalled John Marshall's reminder that Kent Hastings merely worked for Grant. Of course, then, Grant must know exactly what his agent was proposing.

When Kent Hastings had gone, Kelly returned to her desk and sat back in her chair, her eyes closed. The muscles in her shoulders were knotted with tension. She couldn't remember a more emotionally draining day in her entire career. All she wanted was to go back to her room at the hotel, slip under the covers, and sleep. But, she thought as she massaged her neck, she didn't have that sort of luxury. She opened her eyes and forced herself to start going through Grant's contract proposal clause by clause. She was making a mental tally of the total cost of the deal when Janie buzzed and announced that Lyndon was on the line.

"Thanks, Janie," she said, punching the flashing light on her phone. "Mr. Phillips, how are you?"

"How the hell do you think I am?" he bellowed. "My top anchorman and my station manager making a public spectacle of themselves. What in God's name were you thinking of, woman?"

Something in Kelly snapped as Lyndon went on berating her. "Wait just a minute," she interrupted. "You're the one who wanted me to go chasing after Grant Andrews. I should think you'd be thrilled to see your plan in action."

"I told you to do what you had to do to get Grant to sign a new contract. I didn't tell you to do it in the middle of downtown Chicago with the whole blasted world looking on!"

"I'm terribly sorry that your sense of morality was offended," Kelly sputtered sarcastically. "You'll have to pardon me, though, if I have a little trouble figuring out just where you draw the line."

Lyndon quieted down in the face of her outburst. When he spoke again, his tone was calmer. "Okay.

You've made your point. Where do we stand on the contract?"

"I've just finished a meeting with Grant's agent. I'm going over their terms now. As soon as I've had a chance to look at the whole contract, I'll have a better idea of what it's going to take for us to keep him."

"You'll keep me posted?"

"Of course," she said sweetly. "You are the boss."

"I'm glad you remember that," he barked, then slammed down the phone. Kelly shook her head, which was beginning to throb, and went back to work. Within minutes the phone buzzed again.

"Yes, Janie," she said wearily.

"Mr. Andrews is out here. He'd like to see you."

Kelly recalled Kent Hastings's warning. Still, if Grant came to her office, she couldn't very well refuse to see him. "Send him in," she said.

When Grant walked through the door some of the anxiety that had haunted Kelly throughout the day faded away. He was wearing a pair of tan slacks and a crisp white shirt open at the neck. His tie was knotted loosely and his sleeves were rolled up, revealing tanned, muscular forearms. Kelly's mind shifted irrelevantly to an exquisite sculpture by Michelangelo she had seen at the Louvre in Paris. Grant's body had the same powerful impact on her senses. He conveyed the same sort of strength and, in his roughhewn way, a masculine beauty.

"Hi, boss lady," he greeted her, sitting on the edge

of her desk next to her, his leg brushing against her knee. "You look beat."

"Thanks," she retorted. "And you look as though you'd just spent a relaxing weekend at the beach. Mind telling me how you did it?"

He grinned. "And give away one of my secrets for eternal youth? I don't think so," he said doubtfully. "Of course, for the right price I might consider selling it to you."

"What's the price?"

"A kiss."

"I don't know," Kelly replied skeptically. "Kissing you seems to have become a rather expensive proposition lately." She gestured at the contract on her desk. "I've been going over your latest demands."

"I see," he said. "How about if we make this kiss just between us? Our own private fringe benefit?"

"Your agent might disapprove," Kelly warned him lightly. "I've been ordered to stay away from you. He seems to think I'm a bad influence on your image."

"You probably are, but I was getting bored with my image anyway," he said easily.

Expecting to hear a contradiction, Kelly was surprised by Grant's words. "And just what do you mean by that?" she demanded.

"Kent likes to see my name linked with a different woman every week. He thinks it gives all those lonely women in the audience hope that they could be the next in line."

"How accommodating of you to go along with him," Kelly mocked. "I'm sure it's been rough on you."

He looked at her sharply. "Do I detect a note of jealousy?" he teased.

"Don't flatter yourself. You can rotate the entire feminine population of Chicago through your life for all I care. It'll be good for the ratings," she snapped.

"That's what Kent thought," he said, adding in a low, conspiratorial tone, "I also think he likes living vicariously through me. It's the only way he can gawk at a steady parade of gorgeous women without getting into trouble at home. His wife is a tyrant."

Kelly tried to imagine Kent Hastings married to a woman who could dominate him. No wonder the poor man disliked doing business with a female. It probably reminded him all too vividly of his home life, which was probably the only part of his life over which he didn't have total control.

"You wouldn't want to tell me a few of his wife's techniques, would you?" Kelly suggested.

"And have you use them against me in the negotiations?" Grant replied in feigned horror. "Not a chance. But that's a nice try. I think I see why Kent wants you to stay away from me."

"I don't see that I'm such a big threat," Kelly retorted. "I haven't been able to get you to sign your new contract. I haven't even been able to talk you into revealing a single secret."

"That's only because you haven't offered me the right deal," he taunted her, his eyes darkening with the warmth of passion as they roved over her body. "We could start with that kiss now and see what it will get you."

Even as he spoke he was leaning toward her. Kelly knew she was powerless to resist, even if she'd wanted to. His lips brushed lightly across hers, teasing her with their silky touch. His hands clasped hers and he was pulling her up and into his arms. This time when his mouth found hers there was a desperation to his touch, a hunger that held them together in search of fulfillment.

Kelly had the oddest feeling that this embrace would have to last her for a very long time and that feeling made her incredibly aware of every sensation Grant was arousing in her. It was as though she must imprint them on her memory for some lonely time in the future when he would not be with her, when her arms would not be able to circle his waist as they did now.

Her hands crept up and loosened the knot in his tie further, so that she could slip it from around his neck. Then, one by one, she undid the buttons of his shirt until she had access to his bared chest. Her palms rested there on the soft mat of dark hair, beneath which she could feel the steady throbbing of his heart. She buried her face in his shoulder, reveling in the warm, rough feel of his skin against her smooth cheek.

Gently, Grant stroked her back. The touch was meant only to be comforting, but it aroused a flood of white-hot sensations in Kelly just the same. The blood raced through her veins as she realized with a fleeting sense of panic that she wanted to possess and be possessed by Grant right here in the office. It frightened her that her feelings for this man were so powerful, so consuming that she no longer had any control over them. Still trembling from the intensity of her desire, she wrenched herself free from his embrace.

"Kelly?" Grant said, his voice a husky moan. "Don't move away from me now. I want you."

She turned her back on the naked desire she saw in his eyes. "No," she whispered.

He placed his hand on the sensitive nape of her neck, his fingers curling through her tangled hair. "Please."

"I can't." Her voice was a harshly uttered cry. She turned to face him, blinking to keep the tears that filled her eyes from spilling over onto her cheeks.

"Why not?" he wondered, his expression puzzled.

"Because it's not just you and me involved here. Lyndon, your agent, Dean Evans, hell, the whole bloody city can't wait to see what we're going to do next. Lyndon wants me to seduce you. Kent Hastings wants us to stay away from each other. I'm so confused I can't think straight anymore."

"Forget those other people. What do you want? What does Kelly Patrick want?"

"It doesn't matter what I want," she said determinedly. "I've got to think about the station."

"Damn it, Kelly! To hell with the station! We're talking about you and me," Grant exploded.

"There can't be a you and me," she argued, fighting to ignore the pain that felt like a knife twisting in her heart. "Not until we've resolved the contract situation."

"Is this another part of your bargaining strategy? Do you figure if you hold out long enough, I'll be so desperate to get you into bed I'll sign anything?" he demanded derisively. "Well, forget it, honey. You're not that great."

Kelly felt as though he'd slapped her. The vicious words continued to resound in her head as she watched him storm from her office. She had expected him to be angry, but she had not expected him to lash back at her with such calculated cruelty. If he loved her at all, he'd never have been able to say such things to her.

It was just as well, then, that she'd put an end to their embrace as she had. She would make herself forget about Grant, forget about the hours she had spent in his arms. For now she would concentrate only on getting him to sign a new contract. And she would do it strictly by the book, by negotiating with Kent Hastings. She would not allow Grant's image to dance before her as she set the terms. If she did, she would be lost.

CHAPTER ELEVEN

By the time Kelly left the office her head was pounding. She still had hours of work left to do on Grant's contract, and she had no idea how she would manage it when she couldn't seem to keep her mind on anything except the pain in her head and in her heart. With aspirin and a cup of hot tea, she might be able to rid herself of the former, but as far as she could see, there was no cure for the latter. Grant's love might have been a remedy for the emptiness, but he had snatched that away from her the instant he had uttered those heartless words designed to inflict a fatal wound to their relationship. No doubt by tomorrow he would have forgotten all about it. Her replacement would have seen to that.

The thought of Grant with an endless succession of other women renewed the painful throbbing in her head as she walked the few blocks to her hotel. At the lobby desk she was handed a stack of messages, including one from David Stanton inquiring if she was free for dinner. She wondered idly if this had been Lyndon's idea too.

Upstairs in her suite she tossed her briefcase onto the desk and headed straight for the medicine cabinet. When she'd taken a couple of aspirin, she ordered dinner from room service and stretched out on the bed, hoping that a few minutes of rest would get her through the long night still ahead of her. Her eyes had barely closed when the phone rang.

"Yes," she said wearily.

"Kelly?" Grant's voice was low and surprisingly tentative.

"What do you want?"

"I want to talk to you about this afternoon."

"I think I've already heard quite enough from you for today."

"I'm coming over," he insisted.

"Don't bother. I won't let you in."

"Kelly . . ." he began.

"If you have anything to say to me, tell your agent. He can pass it along. He may lack your charm, but at least I always know where I stand with him. Good night," she said firmly, placing the receiver back on the hook. When the phone rang again within minutes, she didn't answer it.

Her dinner arrived a half-hour later and she ate a few bites without really tasting it. With the contract spread out in front of her, she began drafting her counteroffer. She would call Lyndon in the morning to go over the final figures with him, but she was sure he would agree. He wanted Grant too badly not to.

It was after midnight when she finally fell into a restless sleep. Nightmares tormented her throughout the night and more than once she awoke trembling, with only her pillow to hug tightly for comfort. It was a poor substitute for the man she longed to have beside her. Yet each time she thought of Grant she berated herself for the weakness that made her unable to push him from her mind.

Awake at dawn, she took a steaming hot shower, hoping it would wash away some of yesterday's bad memories. She dressed carefully in a tailored suit in a soft shade of dusty rose. Her white blouse had a bow at the neckline and the severe look of her usual upswept hairstyle was softened by a few curly blond wisps that had escaped her bun. The effect would have been one of understated, fragile beauty had it not been for the pallor of her complexion and the pale but unmistakable shadows under her eyes. A careful application of makeup hid some of the ravages of the long night, but nothing could remove the sadness of her eyes.

At the office she waited impatiently until she could safely call Lyndon at home. Unlike her, he was not an early riser and he tended to bark more loudly than usual if his sleep was disturbed.

"What the devil are you doin' callin' me in the middle of the night?" he grumbled when she reached him.

"It is hardly the middle of the night," Kelly replied tartly. "I need to go over Grant's contract with you."

"You going to set that deal today?" he asked, his interest sparking an improvement in his attitude.

"I hope so," she said fervently. Quickly, she spelled out the terms Kent Hastings had demanded and her planned response. Lyndon uttered an occasional expletive at the figures she was tossing about, but when she had finished, he grunted his approval.

"You sure that's the best you can do?"

"I'm going to start lower than that, but I think this is the least they'll settle for."

"Then go with it," he said matter-of-factly. "And, Kelly—"

"Yes."

"You've done a good job with this."

"The contract's not signed yet."

"It will be. To paraphrase an old Bette Davis movie, Kent Hastings won't go for the moon when you're handing him the stars."

"Assuming, of course, that we're offering him enough of them," Kelly agreed with a harsh chuckle.

"I'd say we are," Lyndon predicted, his booming laugh joining hers.

Two hours later Kent Hastings was in her office. His brash, confident attitude was designed to throw Kelly off, but she'd prepared herself for it and she parried his pointed remarks easily. They had just settled themselves at the conference table, papers before them, when Janie came in to announce that Grant was in the outer office and insisted on joining them. Before either of them could speak, he was in the room.

"Grant, I don't think you should be here," Kent

Hastings said in a hushed undertone, giving his client a disapproving look.

"Why not? It's my life you're talking about. I'd like to have some say in what's to be done with it." His eyes met Kelly's, and there was an open challenge in them. "Unless Miss Patrick objects, of course."

Kelly swallowed and shook her head. "Stay if you like. It doesn't matter to me," she said, knowing the words were a lie. It mattered far too much. Her pulse had started racing at the mere sight of him in the doorway, his long legs spread in a defiant stance, his hands shoved into his pockets. He gave her a little half-smile of satisfaction and strolled over to the conference table, pulling out the chair next to hers and settling into it.

Kelly felt as though she were suffocating. It was bad enough that Grant had insisted on being here at all, but to have him so close was unbearable. His knee brushed against her leg under the table and she jumped as though she'd been burned. She tried to inch her chair away from him, but when she caught the victorious expression in his eyes, she forced herself to remain right where she was.

"Shall we get on with this?" she asked, directing the question to Kent Hastings.

"Of course, Miss Patrick," he said, looking at her oddly as he sensed the undercurrents in the room.

Clause by clause they went through the entire deal, Kelly chipping away at his demands until she had reached an acceptable figure. She won more points than she lost, though she was barely aware of her success. Her entire being seemed to be focused on Grant, who remained stonily silent at her side throughout the proceedings. The only sign of his presence was the steady, absentminded drumming of his fingers on the table. The cadence became more rapid as his level of impatience increased. She had a feeling he was about to erupt, but when the explosion came it took her and Kent Hastings by surprise.

"Okay, that's enough!" he shouted, slamming his fist down. "Kent, get out of here!"

A look of shocked disbelief registered on the agent's face. "Grant, what is it?" he asked soothingly. "We're almost finished here. This contract will make you a very wealthy man."

"I don't give a damn about the money or the contract. I want you to leave us alone." When the agent hesitated, he added urgently, "Now!"

"Whatever you say," he said resignedly. "But I think you're making a terrible mistake."

"You don't even know what I'm about to do," Grant charged. "So how can you possibly know whether it's a mistake?"

Flustered by his client's tirade, Kent Hastings got to his feet and gathered his papers together. Kelly almost felt sorry for him, he looked so confused by the sudden turn of events. Apparently Grant sensed that confusion as well, because he finally calmed down and apologized.

"Look, Kent, I'm sorry. I didn't mean to blow up

at you. You've done everything you could for me. Now it's time for me to take over."

The older man nodded, though clearly he still had no idea what was going on. When he had gone, Grant faced Kelly.

"Get your things," he ordered. "We're getting out of here."

"Grant Andrews, I have no intention of leaving this office with you," Kelly replied sharply.

"If you expect to close this deal," he said ominously, "you will get your things together right now." To emphasize his point, he retrieved her briefcase from her desk and began stuffing the contract pages into it. He was making a haphazard jumble of it before she finally relented and took over. "Let me do it, before you ruin the thing," she said, smoothing the rumpled pages.

"Is that it?" he asked when she'd finished.

"Is that what?"

"Is that all you'll need? Don't you have a purse or something?"

"Yes. I have a purse, but I still haven't agreed to go anywhere with you."

"Don't be obstinate, Kelly. You'll come. The only question is whether you'll do it peacefully or whether I'll have to drag you out of here. I'm sure the *Times* would have a field day with that sight."

"You're being a bloody bully, Grant Andrews."

"Yes. I am," he agreed. "You have your tactics. I have mine. Now, are you ready?"

Kelly had no idea how to deal with Grant when

he was in a mood like this. The last thing in the world she wanted was to be alone with him. All of her resolve to keep a safe distance between them could be wiped out with a single touch. Bargaining with Kent Hastings, she had the upper hand. With Grant there was no question about which of them would be negotiating from a position of strength. Damn it, she became weak just being in the same room with him. Every bit of cool, sophisticated business training she'd possessed seemed to drain away in the face of his warm smile. John Marshall had warned her to beware of Kent Hastings's tactics. Hastings, he'd said, could talk her out of the station. That was nothing compared to what Grant could command, she thought, amused by the irony of it. Everyone had thought the agent was the dangerous force in these talks. Instead, it was Grant himself.

"We can't go anywhere," she said at last, trying to keep her voice steady as she borrowed time.

"Why not?" Grant demanded. "What excuse have you come up with now?"

"You have a newscast to do in less than an hour," she pointed out reasonably.

Grant cursed softly under his breath as he went to her desk. Jamming at the push buttons on her phone, he dialed the newsroom and asked for John Marshall.

"John, can you get Bill to take over for me tonight? Something's come up."

Kelly stared at him aghast. "You can't do that," she hissed at him, coming to stand in front of him.

Grant pulled her tightly to his side, his arm like a steel trap around her waist. "Oh, but I can," he said softly, his breath a disturbing whisper against her ear. Into the phone, he said, "Thanks, John. I'm sorry about the short notice, but it couldn't be helped."

"That's totally irresponsible," Kelly charged when he had hung up. "We pay you to go on the air every night, not just when it suits your fancy."

"So, fire me," he suggested calmly, still holding her pressed against him, the contact making her body burn with desire.

"Don't tempt me," she muttered, breaking free so she could put a safe distance between them again. His eyes glinted dangerously at her obvious maneuver, but he elected not to make an issue of it. Instead, he walked to the door, then looked back at her.

"Coming?"

Kelly stared at him defiantly, but at last, giving a gesture of helplessness, she picked up her purse and briefcase and followed him out.

Neither of them said a word as Grant drove through the heavy downtown traffic until he reached an expressway heading northwest out of town.

"Where are we going?" Kelly demanded.

"To dinner," he replied curtly.

"Where?" she repeated. "The way you're driving we'll end up in Canada."

He gave her a scathing look. "What difference does it make? I promise the food will be edible. More important, though, there will not be an entire world there with nothing better to do than interfere in our lives."

"That'll be a pleasant change," Kelly murmured under her breath as the car continued to speed along the unfamiliar road. The Chicago suburbs gave way to rolling countryside and, as the sun streaked the sky with a dazzling shade of orange, Grant turned off in the driveway of an inn, which had been indicated only by a discreet roadside marker. The parking lot of the converted farmhouse was filled with cars bearing tags from several states, proof that the place was hardly a well-kept secret despite its out-of-the-way location.

Kelly stepped out of the car and reached back for her briefcase. "Leave it," Grant ordered.

"You said this was going to be a business meeting," she said stubbornly. "I'll need the contract."

"You won't need anything," he insisted. "I'm sure you have every detail stored away in that brain of yours anyway."

When they entered the bright, airy lobby, it was deserted except for a small, cheerful woman who was working behind the desk. When she saw them, she rushed to greet them.

"Mr. Andrews, it's good to see you again. It's been a while," she said, her weatherbeaten face smiling warmly.

"So much for escaping from your fans," Kelly muttered darkly.

"She's not a fan. She's a friend. I've been here before," Grant hissed back before turning on a full measure of his charm for the woman. "You look as lovely as ever, Mrs. Dowell. How's your husband? I didn't see him outside when we drove up."

"He's in the dining room. He's been working much too hard, as usual," she said, her expression changing to a worried frown. "But he'll be real glad to see you. You go on in."

Miffed at being ignored throughout this exchange and at the thought that Grant was a regular customer at this cozy little inn, Kelly trailed reluctantly along behind him, not bothering to hide her growing irritation. In the dining room there was no mistaking the innkeeper. His nut-brown face was as tanned and wrinkled as his wife's. He was tall and had a loping stride that brought him quickly to where Grant and Kelly waited in the doorway. The hand he held out to Grant was large and calloused, the hand of a man who worked, if anything, even harder than his wife had said. He pumped Grant's hand so enthusiastically, it was all Kelly could do to hide her smile as she saw the newsman wince with pain.

When Grant introduced them, Mr. Dowell grinned shyly at her, reminding her of an awkward teenager. "It's my pleasure, miss," he said softly and with such gentle sincerity that Kelly fell immediately under his spell. By the time he had guided them to a table overlooking a garden filled with a haphazardly planted profusion of bright summer flowers, she was chatting with him as if she'd known him for years. The abrupt lightening of her mood was not lost on Grant. When they were alone, he looked at her wistfully and said, "Do you know what I'd do to have you smile at me like that again?"

"Perhaps if you were as open with me as Mr. Dowell, I would," she told him pointedly. The sharply spoken words apparently hit their mark, because Grant flinched uncomfortably and turned his attention to the menu.

When the waitress came, Kelly ordered vichyssoise, an herbed chicken dish, and fresh broccoli. Grant ordered the beef stew recommended by Mr. Dowell and a salad, along with a bottle of hearty Burgundy. There was already a loaf of crusty homebaked bread on the table and a chilled dish of just-churned butter. Kelly sliced off a thick chunk of the bread just to have something to do. She noted that Grant seemed equally ill-at-ease. He was breaking his slice of bread into small crumbs, more suitable for feeding birds than humans.

At last, when Kelly thought she wouldn't be able to stand another minute of the silence, he asked awkwardly, "Do you like the inn?"

Struck by the inanity of the question, Kelly giggled. Catching the look of confusion that flashed across Grant's face, she tried to smother her laughter. "I'm sorry," she apologized. "It's just that with all we have to talk about, I wasn't ready for you to start by asking whether I approved of your choice of a restaurant."

"It was the safest topic I could think of," he admitted.

Kelly shook her head and regarded him sorrowfully. "Is that what it's come to?" she wondered. "Unless we stick to small talk, we can't communicate?"

"I hope not. I just thought perhaps your mood would improve after a pleasant dinner."

"My mood?" Kelly retorted indignantly. "You're the one who blew up this afternoon and threw your own agent out of my office. Then you practically kidnapped me and dragged me out here."

"I didn't think I had a choice. Everything seemed to be getting out of hand back there. I thought we needed to talk privately and settle this once and for all."

"I've been trying to do that for days," she reminded him.

"So you have, Miss Patrick. So you have," he said wearily. "But I wasn't ready before."

"And you are now?"

"Yes. Unless, of course, you plan to be as bullheaded as usual and refuse to discuss this just because we're not following your timetable."

"Grant Andrews, you are the most infuriating man I have ever met! I have not said one word about not talking. If you're ready to talk now, be my guest. You have my undivided attention."

She watched and waited as he seemed to struggle to find the words he wanted. At last he faced her squarely, his eyes glinting in the flickering candlelight. When he spoke, his voice was firm and had an air of finality about it.

"Okay. When we leave here I'll sign the contract that you and Kent worked out this afternoon."

Kelly's pulse began to race. She had done it! She had finalized the deal and, while it was not exactly what she'd hoped she could get, it was certainly reasonable. Lyndon would be ecstatic.

"Grant, that's—" she began, but he stopped her with a harsh look.

"Wait," he said, "I'm not finished. I will sign the contract on one condition."

Her hopes plummeted. "What condition?"

"That you will pack your things when we get back to town and move in with me," he said without a moment's hesitation. From the look on his face, Kelly knew he meant every word.

How could he do this? How could he tie this damnable contract to their relationship? She could never agree to such a coldblooded proposition. She wanted a lifetime commitment, not some package deal that was linked to Grant's tenure with Phillips Broadcasting.

"And what do I get out of this arrangement?" she asked bitterly. "Will my contract with you run out in five years, just as yours will with the station? Or will you be able to drop my option whenever you please?"

"You'll get to keep your job," he said harshly. "Isn't that enough? That's all these past couple of weeks have been about anyway, isn't it?"

The pain that assailed Kelly at his words was so deep, she couldn't imagine it ever healing. Feeling physically ill, she shoved her chair back from the table and stood up. Trembling with rage, she stared at Grant defiantly.

"You can take your contract and shred it into tiny little pieces for all I care! I'll turn in my resignation tomorrow. I don't even want to be in the same city with you, much less the same station. As for the thought of sharing your bed and board, the idea makes me sick to my stomach," she said, bolting away from the table and running through the dining room. She reached the lobby just in time to hear the first rumblings of thunder. As she ran outside, lightning flashed through the pitch black sky and rain began to fall, first in scattered drops, then in solid, wind-driven sheets.

Soaked, she stumbled on toward the car, praying that it had been left unlocked. She knew it was too much to hope that it would also have the keys in it, but at least it would provide her with shelter until she could figure out what to do. The passenger door was open, testimony to her earlier forgetfulness, and she climbed in. She was still sitting there, shivering in the suddenly cold night air, when Grant joined her.

Teeth chattering, she demanded, "Take me home."

"We're not going anywhere," he replied. "There's a tornado watch on. It's too dangerous."

"Then get out of here and leave me alone."

"Kelly, be reasonable," he said in a placating tone. "Come back inside where it's warm. If you stay out here in those clothes, you'll catch pneumonia."

At the moment that seemed like a pleasant alternative to her tormented mind. "I'll take my chances," she insisted stubbornly.

"Then I'll stay here with you," Grant said, settling more comfortably into the seat.

Kelly couldn't believe it. He was impossible! She was not about to be confined with him in this car another minute. "All right," she said sullenly. "Let's go back inside."

"I thought you might see it my way," he said smugly.

They ran through the downpour to the inn, where Mr. and Mrs. Dowell were both waiting for them, concern evident on their faces.

"Good heavens, you two will catch your death of cold if you don't get out of those clothes," Mrs. Dowell said, clucking over them. "Henry, go upstairs and light a fire in room twelve. I'll bring up a nice pot of hot tea and some sherry. That ought to take the chill off."

Kelly looked at Grant helplessly. "I will not go up there with you," she muttered under her breath.

He shrugged. "Fine. Stay down here and freeze. I'm going up and sit by the fire." He headed for the stairs.

Kelly turned to Mrs. Dowell. "Couldn't I have another room, please?"

"I'm sorry, my dear. That's the only one available. When the weather turned, a number of people decided to stay for the night." Seeing Kelly's crestfallen expression, she suggested, "I suppose you could go sit by the fire in the dining room for a while. Most of the guests have gone to their rooms."

"Thanks," Kelly said gratefully, following Mrs. Dowell back to the dining room.

It was true. The room was nearly empty now and the blazing fire beckoned with its promised warmth. Kelly went over and sat huddled in front of it, watching the flames dance. As it crackled, she kept seeing Grant's face flickering before her with the elusiveness of a ghost's image. His demand that she move in with him echoed in her mind, mocking the emotions he had stirred in her. She had dared, for the first time in her life, to love. That love had brought her nothing but unbearable pain. Never, she promised herself with conviction, never would she allow herself to become so vulnerable again.

CHAPTER TWELVE

Kelly wasn't sure how long she'd been asleep when she awakened abruptly with the desolate, empty feeling that sometimes comes after a bad dream. Massaging her stiff muscles, she moved closer to the dying embers of the fire and tried to recall what she'd been dreaming about. Grant had been at the center of it, she knew, just as he had been at the center of her existence for days now. But in her nightmare he had been walking away, and, no matter how fast she ran or how loudly she called to him, he refused to turn back. Rubbing her hand across her cheeks, she realized with surprise that they were damp, apparently from tears she had shed during the dream.

"Kelly?" The voice was soft and low, but it was unmistakably Grant's. She looked across the dining room and saw him framed in the doorway, as though unsure about whether he should come any closer. Although her stomach tightened at the sight of him, she clenched her hands in her lap and willed herself to remain silent. He would have to make the decision to approach her entirely on his own. She was not about to give him any encouragement, not after last night.

Slowly, silently, he made his way across the room and sat down beside her. "How are you feeling?" he asked finally.

"Fine," she told him curtly, refusing to meet his gaze.

"I don't believe you," he said quietly.

"What's new about that?" she responded bitterly.

"Kelly, please," he implored her, putting his hand lightly on her arm. At the contact with the still-damp sleeve of her blouse, his manner changed abruptly from one of supplication to gruff anger. "Good God, you're soaking wet. I want you to come upstairs right now. You need a hot shower. While you're taking one, I'll get your things dried out."

"Forget it. I'll survive."

"Maybe. If you stop behaving like a damn fool and get upstairs."

"I am not going to that room with you," she insisted stubbornly.

"Kelly, you will either stand up right this minute and come with me or I'll pick you up and carry you!"

She faced him, then, her eyes blazing with fury and her voice icy, and she said, "If you put one hand on me, Grant Andrews, I'll raise such a ruckus, this entire inn will think a tornado blew through."

"You wouldn't dare," he challenged, his features taking on a hard, determined set.

"Try me," she taunted.

"Okay," he said slowly, regarding her as he might

a difficult child. "Have it your way," he muttered, scooping her into his arms and striding across the room.

Kelly was so startled by the speed with which he moved that it took her a minute to react. Then she pounded her fists against his chest and tried frantically to twist out of his grasp. But Grant had braced himself for the attack and warded it off as if it were nothing more than a slight nuisance. Infuriated by the futility of her struggle, she opened her mouth to yell, but before she could utter a sound, Grant's mouth was against hers, muffling the outcry. Effectively silenced and restrained, she tried to think of other ways to fight the hold he had on her, but then the bruising touch of his lips began to arouse an entirely different sort of primitive reaction. Her outrage, her instinctive response to the danger he represented rapidly gave way to the beginnings of desire. The flames of passion flickered to life, threatening to engulf her in their fiery heat.

Angry at her body's weakness, she tried to ignore the sensations created by the persistent movement of his lips, the darting forays of his tongue. This, too, was a hopeless struggle. As though they had a will of their own, her arms curved around his shoulders and she nestled more tightly against his chest. Now, when his tongue teased at her lips, they parted to allow him entrance and her own tongue flicked lightly against his teeth before penetrating beyond.

They were both breathless by the time they reached the room on the inn's second floor, but

Grant somehow managed to keep her locked tightly against him as he opened the door and carried her into the room. At last, with obvious reluctance, he put her down gently on the bed. Kelly looked at him expectantly, thinking he would join her. Instead, he backed away.

Still breathing raggedly, either from the exertion of bringing her upstairs or from their prolonged kiss, he ordered her harshly, "Get undressed and get into the shower." His tone allowed no room for argument and he kept his back to her as he moved across to stare out the window at the lingering storm. Unwilling to accept his command, Kelly came up behind him and wrapped her arms around his waist, pressing herself against his back.

"Grant," she appealed in a low, provocative voice.

Stiffening visibly against her assault on his senses, he repeated firmly, "Go take a hot shower."

Stung by this unexpected rejection, she turned away so that he wouldn't glimpse the tears that threatened to spill from her eyes. Trying to inject a flippant note into her voice, she mocked, "Maybe I'd better make that a cold shower."

It was only after she was in the bathroom with the water pounding against her aching muscles that she allowed the tears to flow unchecked. *Just let me get through the rest of this night,* she prayed silently. *Then I'll find a way to never see him again.* She tried to choke back the sobs that made her shake so violently that she had to lean against the cool tiles of the shower stall to steady herself.

When, at last, the crying was over, she turned off the water and grabbed one of the thick towels to dry herself. It wasn't until she had rubbed her hair until it curled about her head like a golden halo that she realized her clothes were gone. What the devil was she supposed to do now? Wrapping herself in one of the remaining towels, she peeked into the bedroom and saw with relief that Grant was gone. Quickly she ran to the bed and slipped under the covers, snuggling beneath the welcome warmth. As a pleasant languor stole over her, she wondered momentarily what had become of Grant, but within minutes she had pushed those thoughts from her mind and fallen into a sound, dreamless sleep. Exhaustion had brought her a reprieve from the night's turmoil.

When she awoke hours later the first gray light of dawn was casting morning shadows about the room. A heavy weight seemed to hold her pinned to the bed and, blinking away the fuzziness of sleep, she saw that Grant was beside her, lying fully clothed on top of the covers, one leg tossed across hers, an arm curved around her waist. She tried to inch away without waking him, but each tiny movement of her body only made him tighten his grasp. At last, accepting her imprisonment, she relaxed and allowed herself the fleeting luxury of enjoying his protective embrace.

How could she give him up, she wondered as she studied his sleeping profile. Could she ever willingly abandon all future moments of closeness, of having him hold her, touch her, possess her? Her heart seemed to constrict in her chest at the thought of it. She loved this man, loved him in all of the trite, clichéd ways ever written about in popular songs, romantic movies, and novels. Knowing that, perhaps she should simply swallow her pride and accept his offer. At least then they would be together. If it didn't last, so be it. She would have had a few weeks, a few months of knowing what it was like to wake with Grant beside her, to share the little intimacies of daily life with someone she loved.

Grant stirred beside her, his hand shifting ever so slightly to cover her breast. Kelly's breath caught in her throat as his fingers began to trace circles around the tautening peak. His gentle manipulation continued until the nipple had hardened and each touch sent an electric current of pleasure through her body.

When a soft moan escaped her lips, Grant rolled her willing body toward him, allowing him access to all of her most vulnerable points of arousal. His touch became increasingly insistent as he sought her ultimate surrender and, finally, she gave in, arching her body toward his, no longer a passive partner in the lovemaking he had initiated.

With anxious hands she began removing the clothes that kept her from the warmth and roughness of his skin. When she'd opened the buttons of his shirt, the material fell away from his chest, allowing her to trail her fingers lazily through the mat of hairs that created a dark shadow between his pebble-hard nipples. While Grant continued to stroke her breasts, her hips, and the soft, sensitive skin of her inner thighs, she struggled to unbuckle his belt and free him of his slacks.

When, at last, there were no longer any barriers between them, their movements took on a desperate urgency. Their breathing accelerated and Kelly felt as though her skin were on fire. Each time it brushed against Grant's, that fire seemed to rage out of control.

"Kelly, I want you," Grant whispered, his voice thick with desire. "I want to love you."

"Yes. Please," Kelly moaned in response. "Please, love me." She knew she was pleading for far more than these few moments of physical pleasure, and yet, for the moment, it was enough to be lost to his touch.

She urged her body toward his, thrilling at the hard, thrusting contact that was taking them to ever-spiraling heights. Her fingers dug into his back as he lifted her toward a peak of sensations she had never believed possible. When the mounting tension was just this side of unbearable, together they were swept over the edge into the ultimate, shattering release. Grant's name was on Kelly's lips at that moment, murmured against his damp shoulder as she clung to him. She knew then, if she hadn't before, that she could never bear to let him go, no matter what the price. She would stay with him on his terms until he forced her out of his life.

Shifting her body so that it was next to his, her arm across his stomach, her head resting on his shoulder, she took a deep breath.

"Grant," she began softly.

"Yes," he said, his hand idly stroking her hair.

"If . . . if you still want me to, I'll move in with you."

At her words, he froze. "Is that what you want?" he asked, his voice surprisingly stiff and cold.

Kelly wanted to tell him no, that she wanted so much more, but she said only, "It's what I want."

"Fine," he said briskly, taking her at her word. "We'll pick your things up when we get back to town." With that, he climbed out of the bed, picked up his clothes, and stalked into the bathroom.

Kelly stared after him in dismay. What on earth had she said to make him so furious? Wasn't this what he wanted? It had been his idea, for heaven's sake!

"Blast him," she muttered angrily, wanting to throw something. Instead, she took out her frustration on the pillow, pummeling it with her fist.

When Grant returned, his hair still damp from his shower, she watched him wearily, trying to gauge his mood. Judging that his temper seemed to have improved somewhat, she dared a question. "Grant, don't you want me to move in with you after all?"

"Yes, damn it," he snapped.

"Then what's wrong?"

"Nothing," he replied curtly. "Get dressed so we can get out of here."

Throwing her hands up in a gesture of defeat, Kelly murmured furiously, "Anything you say, master. I don't suppose you'd like to get my clothes so I can do that."

"I had Mrs. Dowell dry them last night. They're in the closet," he informed her, walking to the door. "I'll wait for you downstairs."

Kelly stared after him in amazement. This time when the urge to throw something came over her, she did. The plastic ashtray she grabbed hit the door with a loud crack and fell to the carpet, still in one piece. Perhaps that's an omen, she thought. Maybe they could survive this latest round of absurd hostility without shattering as well.

Kelly took her time getting ready to leave. In part her delay was due to her obstinate refusal to allow Grant to order her around. Just as important, though, was her unwillingness to subject herself to any more of his puzzling outbursts. When she finally did go downstairs, he was pacing around the lobby in long, angry strides.

"What took you so long?" he demanded, giving her a look of reproach.

"I had to call the office and let them know I wouldn't be in until later," she informed him calmly, adding, "You might be interested to know that Lyndon and your agent have been calling every half-hour to see if we've reached an agreement."

"I suppose you told Janie to inform them that you've got your damn agreement."

"I did not."

He regarded her curiously. "Why not? I thought

you couldn't wait for the chance to start gloating about it."

Ignoring his tone, she said, "First of all, you haven't signed anything yet. And, if and when you do, I think it's something we ought to tell them ourselves."

"I'm sure you're right," he sneered. "It wouldn't do for the big news to leak out too soon, not when you can orchestrate a big publicity splash by waiting for the right moment." He marched out the door without waiting to see whether she would follow. Kelly was tempted to stay right where she was, but common sense told her it was pointless to antagonize him any further. His mood was already foul enough.

They made the long drive back into town in silence. Kelly stole an occasional glimpse sideways, but Grant's face remained stonily impassive, his eyes never wavering from the road. For two people about to start a life together, they were certainly off to a wonderful start, she thought wryly. She could hardly wait until they really had a fight about something.

When they arrived at her hotel, Grant followed her to her suite without a word. Then, like a sentry who'd been posted to assure her compliance with their bargain, he stood by as she began gathering her things. No matter where she moved in the room, his eyes seemed to follow her, condemning her in some way she could not fathom. She wanted to scream, to shout just to break the awkward quiet that hung in the air, making it thick with tension.

Working first to clear out the desk, she found that her hands were shaking so badly she had difficulty stacking the books and papers she wanted to take with her. Just as she added the last book to the pile, she knocked it over, scattering it in every direction. Blinking back tears of anger and confusion, she kneeled to clean up the mess, but Grant was instantly beside her, pushing her fumbling hands out of the way.

"I'll do it," he said impatiently, his own hands sure and steady as they made quick work of reassembling the scattered books and papers. Kelly's mute look of appeal was ignored and eventually she shook her head and got to her feet.

"I'll get my clothes," she said quietly, moving quickly into the bedroom before he could catch sight of the pain she knew was reflected in her eyes.

She ought to back out of this charade now, she thought as she pulled her suitcases from the closet and began filling them with her clothes. She knew, though, that she couldn't do it and that knowledge infuriated her.

Why in God's name am I putting up with this? she demanded of herself as she tossed lingerie, sweaters, blouses, suits, dresses, and shoes into the open luggage. *Because I am a bloody, lovesick fool,* she admitted, eyeing the sloppy packing job she was doing ruefully. She'd probably have to spend a fortune on pressing and dry cleaning.

In the bathroom she removed the jars of makeup and toiletry items from the drawers and medicine cabinet and put them into the small traincase she'd brought in with her. She paused only long enough to apply a light touch of blusher to her pale cheeks and to dab her favorite perfume on her wrists and behind her ears. She hoped this small concession to her vanity would help to boost her confidence for whatever was ahead.

At last, after a final check of the drawers and closets, she was ready. With two of the smaller suitcases in hand, she returned to the living room.

"I'm ready," she announced, looking around for Grant. He wasn't in the room.

"Grant?" she murmured in confusion as she put the luggage down with a soft thud. Standing silently in the middle of the floor, she listened for some sound that would tell her where Grant was. There wasn't a noise coming from anywhere in the entire suite.

He must have gone downstairs to have the car brought around, she decided, when a check of all the rooms proved he was, in fact, gone. She sat on the edge of a chair by the phone to wait.

As the minutes ticked away, she realized with a devastating certainty that he wasn't coming back.

"I don't understand," she whispered aloud, looking around the room in search of clues that would explain his departure. At last her glance came to rest on the stack of books and papers he'd placed back on the desk. Her briefcase, now open, was beside them. Reluctantly, fearing what she would discover, Kelly crossed the room and scanned the neatly arranged material. There, right on top where she couldn't miss it, was her answer. It was the contract. With nervous fingers, she flipped to the final page and found, as she knew she would, Grant's signature.

CHAPTER THIRTEEN

With a stunned sense of disbelief, Kelly picked up the contract and held it in her trembling hands. Grant had actually signed it and then walked out on her without a word. Her mind wrestled with the awful implications, but refused to accept any of them. It couldn't be over. Not like this. And, yet, what other possible explanation could there be? She couldn't think of one as she carefully put the contract back into the briefcase where it would be safe.

Methodically, then, she went about returning her clothes to the drawers and hangers from which she'd only a short time earlier removed them. She accomplished the task with robotlike efficiency, refusing to allow herself to think about what came next. For her, right now, there was no future, only a present filled with an incredible heartache.

In the midst of her anguish, the part of her that had been trained to behave responsibly no matter what reminded her that she was still expected at the office. Managing to keep her voice steady, she offered

Janie what she hoped was a plausible excuse for her absence.

"What should I do about Mr. Phillips and Mr. Hastings?" the secretary inquired anxiously. "I've been putting them off all day."

"You can tell them I'm out of the office for the rest of the day and that I'll get back to them tomorrow."

"Sure, Miss Patrick."

"Thanks, Janie. I'll see you in the morning."

Kelly hung up and drifted back into the living room, just in time to hear the phone ring. She tried to ignore its persistent cry, but the caller was obviously not planning to give up. Reluctantly, she answered it.

"Kelly? You okay?" Lyndon's voice blasted out at her in a tone that blended concern and irritation.

"I'm just fine, Mr. Phillips," she lied smoothly.

"Damn it all, woman, if you're fine, then why aren't you over at the station nailing down that deal with Andrews? And why do you sound like you've lost your best friend?" he added grumpily.

"To answer your questions in order: Grant's already signed the contract and, you're right, I may have lost my best friend," she replied in a voice devoid of emotion.

"You mean you closed that deal?" Lyndon repeated, seizing on the first part of her response.

"Yes and, if you don't mind, I don't want to discuss it right now. I'll call you later," she promised, ignoring the torrent of words that poured from the phone as she hung up. When it rang again, she covered it with a cushion from the sofa and then curled up in one of the armchairs across the room, where the ringing sounded only like a distant memory.

She sat like that for hours, until the room was shrouded in darkness and the emptiness inside her seemed so much a part of her that she felt as though it had always been there. In some dim recess of her consciousness, she heard the phone ringing again and again, but she couldn't think of anyone she wanted to talk to. Nor did she answer the door when the buzzer sounded. Not even when she thought she heard Grant's voice accompanied by a loud pounding on the door did she move from the chair. When it stopped eventually, she felt an odd sense of relief.

Through it all her mind kept replaying the events of the past twenty-four hours. She knew that somewhere there was a key to unlock the mystery of Grant's disappearance, if only she could find it. But, no matter how hard she tried, the answer wouldn't come to her. It remained as elusive as he did.

It was only when she heard the sound of a key in the lock that she managed to shake off her lethargy. Startled into a state of nervous anticipation, she watched in fascination as the knob slowly turned and the door opened.

"Kelly?" Grant's voice had an edge of panic to it. "Kelly, are you in here?"

He flipped on the lights, but it was several seconds before his gaze reached her, where she remained huddled like a small, frightened animal. "Kelly," he said again more softly, coming toward her. She shook her head and held out her hand as though to prevent him from coming any closer.

"I don't want to see you," she told him harshly.

"Honey, we have to talk," he said patiently. "I have to explain."

"I don't want to hear any more of your explanations," she insisted hysterically. "I just want you to get out of here!"

"I'm not leaving," he responded calmly, sitting down across from her to emphasize the point. "I'm staying right here until we've worked this out."

"There is nothing left to work out, Mr. Andrews," she said, biting off the words. "I have played enough emotional games with you in the last few weeks to last me a lifetime. Can't you just take your contract and find some other woman's head to mess with? If you stay in the newsroom and I stay in my office, surely we can manage to coexist with as little pain as possible."

He studied her intently. "Is that what you really want?"

"What I really want doesn't matter anymore," she said, unable to keep a trace of wistfulness from her voice.

Sensing the ambivalence in her attitude toward him, Grant quickly closed the gap separating them and sat on the floor beside her chair. He took her hand in his, holding it loosely so that she had the option of removing it. When she didn't, he said tenderly, "It matters to me, Kelly. I need to know what you're thinking, what you're feeling."

She watched him cautiously, wondering whether she could trust the sincerity she heard in his voice or the look of pain that clouded his eyes. "I thought you already knew," she told him slowly.

"I thought I did too," he admitted. "But maybe I got it all wrong."

Kelly knew that to tell him the truth would mean taking a risk. It would mean exposing herself to possible ridicule. It would also mean allowing him to see more clearly than ever how very vulnerable she had become where he was concerned.

And yet she reminded herself with a faint stirring of optimism that honesty now could also bring an end to the confusion that had marked their entire relationship. It could be the beginning of a new, open communication that would erase their doubts forever. If that happened, the risk would be worth it.

"I want you," she said simply, her words filled with all the love and longing she had been so careful to hide. "I care about you more than I've ever cared about another human being. I want to be with you. I want to have the chance to try to make you happy."

"And that's all?" he prodded, his skepticism reflected in the set of his rugged features as well as in his words.

Responding to the uncertainty in his voice, Kelly swore solemnly, "That's all."

"Is that why you agreed to move in with me?"

She nodded. "It wasn't the way I wanted it to be for us," she confessed, "but your damned coldblooded offer was better than nothing."

The pain in Grant's eyes increased at her admission and he squeezed her hand so hard it hurt. When she could bear his torment no longer, she said quietly, "Now it's my turn."

"Okay."

"Why did you insist that I move in with you in return for signing the contract?"

"Because that was the only way I could think of to be sure you would agree to be with me," he told her guiltily. "I thought once you were in my apartment, once we were together, I could make you learn to love me as much as I love you."

The declaration reverberated in Kelly's head and a heartbeat seemed to skip joyously as she took in its meaning. "You love me?" she repeated softly, as if she couldn't believe what she had heard.

"Boss lady, I've loved you ever since you told me off at Lyndon's party that first night. There you were on that balcony with the lights of Chicago dancing behind you. You were so lovely, so fragile-looking, and yet you made damn sure that I knew you had a will of iron.

"I knew right then that I had to have you, but that contract kept cropping up at every turn. I finally decided to use it to my advantage."

"By blackmailing me into moving in with you?" she accused him, though there was no anger in her words.

"Yes," he conceded sorrowfully. "Think you can ever manage to forgive me?"

"Only if you'll explain why you left here without me, after going to all that trouble."

He laughed. "I guess I'm not as tough as you are. I drove a hard bargain and then I realized I'd never be able to live with myself if I forced you to go through with it. Maybe I should have let Kent negotiate the deal for me."

Kelly slid from the chair to his lap. "Forget it," she advised. "In your case I'll only negotiate with the principal party." She trailed her fingers along the side of his face, then on to his lips. Her mouth slowly followed the same path, finally meeting his in a searing kiss that sealed their bargain.

"How much longer before we have to go through this again?" he asked breathlessly.

"Five years."

He nibbled at her ear as his hands began an urgent quest along her midriff, stopping only when they'd reached her rounded breasts. "That ought to be just about long enough," he murmured.

"Long enough for what?" Kelly asked, gasping as he moved his hands along her abdomen.

"To do this," he said, intensifying his idle touch. "And," he added almost casually, "to get married."

Kelly's eyes sparkled with love as they met his. "Are you sure that's what you want, Grant?"

"Honey, I've never been more certain of anything in my life." Suddenly he paused and regarded her intently. "You don't have any doubts, do you?"

"Only one," she said, and the concern in her voice was only partially feigned.

"What's that?"

"What happens when your ratings drop and I have to fire you?"

"Sweetheart, *if* my ratings drop, it'll be all your fault for removing me from the city's most-eligible-bachelors list. So I guess you'll just have to support me."

"Either that or give you a job in the mail room," she agreed with a grin. Then her expression sobered. "Actually, it's not such a ridiculous question, Grant. What if something like that happens?"

"We can't worry about all the what-ifs, Kelly. We'll just have to take it a step at a time. My job has certain risks. They wouldn't be any different if someone else were the boss. If the ratings fall, you'll do what you have to do, just as anyone else would."

"And we can survive that?"

"We've survived all of Lyndon's schemes, haven't we? That ought to say something about the strength of this relationship."

Suddenly Kelly chuckled.

"What's so funny?"

"I was just thinking about the look on Lyndon's face when he finds out about this. He's going to hit the roof. I don't think this was exactly part of his plan."

"Oh, I don't know," Grant retorted cynically. "This was probably just what he had in mind. Five years from now, when my contract is up, he'll be able to manipulate me at the bargaining table and he'll have you to work on me at home. I won't stand a chance."

Kelly's hands slid along the hard muscles of his thighs and her lips skimmed lightly across the bare skin of his chest, visible above the deep V of his open collar. "You mean this works?" she asked innocently as his breath began to come in ragged gasps.

"Just like this does," he responded, placing her on the floor and pinning her down with his body as he expertly stripped her of her clothes. As each piece came off, his mouth covered the exposed flesh with warm, gentle kisses. By the time she was bared to his cherishing gaze, she was quivering with unparalleled excitement, demanding that he complete their union.

"Love me, Grant," she whispered. "Love me always the way you do tonight."

Moving to do as she asked, he whispered, "That goes without saying, boss lady."

LOOK FOR NEXT MONTH'S
CANDLELIGHT ECSTASY ROMANCES ®